Jane Elizabeth Holmes Jerram

Esther

A Poem

Jane Elizabeth Holmes Jerram

Esther
A Poem

ISBN/EAN: 9783337398231

Printed in Europe, USA, Canada, Australia, Japan

Cover: Foto ©Andreas Hilbeck / pixelio.de

More available books at **www.hansebooks.com**

ESTHER

A Poem

BY

JANE ELIZABETH HOLMES

LONDON

TRESIDDER, 17 AVE MARIA LANE, E.C.

1865

PREFACE.

WHATEVER may be the character of the reception given to this Poem by the critics or the public, it cannot affect the authoress, who is far removed beyond the reach of all human praise or blame.

About two years after writing the last lines of ' ESTHER, ' Miss HOLMES, then in the twenty-fifth year of her age, to the deep distress of her family, and the sincere regret of all who knew her, ceased to be on earth. Their sorrow, however, was greatly mitigated by a knowledge of the fact that she died, as she lived, in the faith of the Gospel. Her temper naturally sweet, and her manners gentle and graceful, adorned as they were by the higher excellences of Christian holiness, rendered her greatly endeared and universally beloved.

Without professing to give a biography of

a

Miss Holmes in this brief Preface, it may be stated that her father, a Leeds merchant, died before she was nine years of age. Much of her childhood was spent at her maternal grandfather's, the late Mr. Timothy Hackworth, of Shildon, near Darlington; a remarkable man, to whose mechanical genius, as the 'father of locomotive engines,' sufficient justice has not yet been done. Her school-days were passed in the neighbourhood of the English lakes, where the scene of this Poem is laid.

Miss Holmes' family, in giving this production of her pen to the public, have no apology to offer. If they did not think it worthy of publication, they would not have sent it to the press. At the same time, it is confessed that a knowledge of the authoress's intentions in this respect has had considerable weight with them in the decision to which they have come.

It would have been a pleasing task to the writer of these prefatory remarks (who is unconnected with the family) to point out some of the peculiar excellencies, both in description and in sentiment, to be found in the following lines. This, however, he leaves to the discriminating reader, who, no doubt, will make the discovery for himself.

The genius of Miss Holmes, unlike that of her grandfather, was not applied to utilitarian purposes. Adam Smith, had he lived to the present, would have placed ' ESTHER ' in the class of 'unproductive labour ; ' while very different would have been his estimate of Timothy Hackworth's ' Royal George '—the first engine furnished with his important invention, the blast-pipe ; and of his ' Sanspareil,' * now in the Kensington Museum. And yet, some readers, despite the ' Wealth of Nations,' pleased with the imaginative in literature, and stirred by the emotional, struck with the descriptive power of this Poem, affected by its tenderness and pathos, and charmed with the purity of sentiment pervading the whole, will rise from its perusal in admiration of the writer, and mention gratefully the name of JANE ELIZABETH HOLMES.

DARLINGTON : *April* 1865.

---

* Which competed for the 500*l*. premium on the Manchester and Liverpool Railway in 1829.

ESTHER.

PART FIRST

'Twas morning, and the sunshine fair
Was falling softly ev'rywhere;
The mountain heights, yet tipp'd with snow,
Were dazzling in its brilliant glow;
It rested on the forest deep,
And up its sombre paths would peep;
Each tall and stately ancient tree
Smiled gaily in its company,
While tiny leaflets all around
Were whisp'ring secrets most profound,
And nodding in the light spring breeze
To friendly leaves on neighb'ring trees.
The brook that wailed the night before,
And moan'd along, now moaned no more,
But danced and sported in its glee,
And sang its song right merrily,
Telling its gladness to the sun,
Its sorrows to the gentle moon.

Not only on the woodland shade,
Or mountain crest or streamlet, played
Those merry sunbeams;—glancing far,
And unrestrained by bolt or bar,
They visited the homes of men,
And waken'd cities once again.
Softly, how softly, they would creep
To rouse the children from their sleep—
Gently reminding them 'twas day,
And bidding them come out to play.
The aged felt their youth renewed,
Their pulses quickened as they stood,
Pleased to inhale the morning air,
And gaze upon a scene so fair ;
While brave, true workers rose again,
To do their part as earnest men ;
And idlers blush'd to waste away
The precious hours of such a day.
The young and gay felt life was sweet,
And hasten'd forth its joys to meet ;
To feel their own hearts' gladsomeness
Augmented by the general bliss :
Thousands, who laid them down to rest,
Burdened with cares, by doubts opprest,
Awoke to feel their load was gone,
Or seemed a very little one ;
For hopes were theirs, instead of fears,
And smiles had quite displaced their tears,

Nor on their spirits weighed a care,
More heavily than they could bear.
The promise still stands lovingly,
That as thy days, thy strength shall be;
And few there are in woful plight
To whom hope comes not with the light;
Whose desolation and despair
Yield nothing with the morning air,—
Commend them to His pitying love,
Who only can their griefs remove,—
Who only can the storm control,
Or speak a peace into the soul.
Giver of ev'ry perfect gift,
To Thee in praise our hearts we lift,
That joys for which our spirits yearn,
Are giv'n to us with day's return;
For hope renewed, and sunshine bright,
We bless Thee, and for morning light!

Close by a lake in Westmoreland,
A stately mansion used to stand:
The fabric may have long laid low,—
For this was many years ago,—
But, on the morn of which I write,
It reared its walls a lofty height.
Within a chamber in the wing,
A maiden fair was slumbering;

Till, through the lattice, sunny beams
Came softly breaking on her dreams.
Oh ! ere she wakes, a moment gaze
Upon that sweet and girlish face :
Earnest and peaceful is her brow,
As if she might be thinking now ;
Her light brown hair, drawn back and twined,
Is gently by the comb confined ;
The eyelids hide her eyes from view,
But they are of a violet blue ;
Their lashes rest upon a cheek,
Whose soften'd colour seems to speak
Of buoyant health and merry play,
On many a welcome holiday ;
For the lips tell she 's but a child,
Light-hearted, petulant, and wild ;
From every sorrow far removed,
And only made to be beloved.
'T was oftener said in waking hours,
By those who knew her girlish powers,
And felt of her rebukes afraid,
That she was made to be obeyed.
A darling child, the only one,
Wilful and restive she had grown ;
Nor would she for a moment brook
The least restraint in word or look,
From any but her parents' hand,—
Obedient to their least command.

Reproof her heart had almost broken;
But such reproof was never spoken.
And rarely was command addressed,
Or aught beyond a wish expressed,
To one that they both loved so well,—
Docile with them, and tractable.
Sometimes, perchance, she 'd condescend
To play the patronising friend
To the poor cottagers around,
Whose homes her father's hall surround;
But those who thus secured her grace
Must deem themselves a favoured race.
She had a gentle courtesy,
And loved was, when she chose to be;
But if her will was slightly crossed,
Courtesy to the winds was tossed,
And passion raged within her soul,
Too oft without the least control.
'T was true her anger did not last,
The fitful cloud was quickly past;
Still, far too clearly you might trace ⎫
The pride of all her haughty race ⎬
Stamped upon Esther Stafford's face. ⎭
Yet true and noble was her heart,
And brave and strong to bear its part,
And promises had budded forth
Of goodness and superior worth;
But some feared that they seemed to be
Half with'ring in prosperity.

Now lightly from her couch she springs,
And dressing quickly, sometimes sings;
Then pausing she would stand and smile,
Communing with herself the while.

  ' And so, 't is sixteen years to-day
Since I was born, the people say.
I 'm glad 't was in the sweet spring time,
Before the year has reached its prime;
I 'm glad 't was near the mountain rills,
Beneath the shadow of the hills;
I 'm glad the joys of life to share,
For earth is very, very fair.
Sixteen ! I'm quite a woman grown,
And that I know my father 'll own;
And Donald Ross shall do the same,
Even from him, I'll homage claim,
Though he seems very proud and stern,
A lady's power he needs to learn;
And little right I trow has he
So haughtily to lecture me,
As he has sometimes dared to do—
Yet I can tell he loves me too.
He but a poor Scotch architect!
'T were fine fun some day to reject
His proffered love, if he should dare
To offer me a gift so rare:
For being poor I would not scorn,—
His poverty is nobly worn.

Yet I could almost taunt him with it,
He chafes me so much by his merit;
That calm contempt I cannot brook,
Which I see often in his look;
His eyes reproaches constant speak,
Bringing the crimson to my cheek;
For though I 've saucy answers made,
Yet of his frown I 'm half afraid.
Then, to be rated and controlled,
Not for ten thousand mines of gold
Would I consent to be his wife,
Or lead such a poor slavish life.'
Suddenly, blushing deepest red,
' I ought to be ashamed,' she said,
' Of thoughts so wrong, and mean, and low.
If Donald knew, he 'd not be slow
To ridicule my fancied power,
Or it might move his pity more;
For one so solemn, grand, and cool,
Could scarcely stoop to ridicule.
But I must hasten my attire,
Or I shall have to meet their ire;
We 'll not be back by breakfast time,
Already six the bells do chime.'
She 'd promised, on the night before,
To row along towards Lyulph's tower,
With Donald and his sister Jessie
(A fair-haired winsome little lassie,

Something of Esther's age and size,
A friend too she did dearly prize)—
They, to return and spend the day,
For 't was to be a holiday.

Before she left her room she knelt,
To breathe a prayer, too little felt.
Poor child !—her life one summer's day,—
She scarcely knew what 't was to pray;
But hurriedly now whispered o'er
Words, which her mother taught of yore;
Then swiftly sped the gallery round,
And down the staircase lightly wound.
She stood a moment lingering
To hear her favourite linnet sing
Congratulations most sincere,
That she had reach'd her sixteenth year.
She could not but supply its need,
Of water pure, and wholesome seed;
While Wallace, pulling at her dress,
Impatiently claim'd his caress.
As soon as e'er the bird was fed,
She stooped, and fondly stroked his head,
And he, well gratified but mute,
Tendered his ev'ry day salute :
Shaking the paw the dog extended,
She gravely hoped his health was mended,

Then quickly springing up again,
Went scamp'ring with him down the lane.

Already seated in the boat,
And wrapped in most unwonted thought,
Or 'tranced by reverie's witching spell
(A power that all have proved full well)—
Jessie flung idly from her hand
Pebbles she 'd gathered on the strand,
Into the bosom of the lake,
To watch the eddying curls they 'd make.
It might be, that her thoughts had flown
To friends whose memory alone
Was treasured now within her breast;
To joys that she had once possessed,
When sporting with her sisters three,
In childhood's home beside the sea,
That softly kissed old Scotland's shore;
Joys that might come no more—no more.
Now left alone to Donald's care,
With none besides her love to share,
It might be she was castle building,
With rosy hues their future gilding;
For Jessie's thoughts were apt to hide,
And revel on the sunny side
Of life,—if sunshine could be found,
'T was with her musings interwound.

Dream on, young hearts, as guilelessly !
For oh ! if life's reality
Ever surpass the dreams of youth,
Hope brightening into actual truth,
Joys, coming fast, without one cross,
'Twould be to such as Jessie Ross.
I would not say such dreams must be
Illusive, fleeting vanity;
But should they all be doom'd to perish,
Say, who would sternly cease to cherish
Things so beguiling, fair, and gay ?
Who would not rather bid them stay,
Adorning life with added beauties,
Not interfering with its duties?

Upon the pebbly beach there stood,
Protected by the sylvan wood,
And glancing sideways at the lake,
A fairy cot, of gothic make ;
Above its head, in fond embrace,
The giant trees did interlace
Their boughs, now clad with foliage green ;
To shed new lustre on the scene,
The rose and jessamine combined,
As up the walls and porch they twined.
Leaning against the rustic gate,
Stood Donald Ross, to watch and wait,

For Esther's bounding step to come,
Hastily racing towards his home.
Some thirty years he might have past,
Exposed to many a bitter blast;
Rather above the middle height,
Of active form, well knit but slight;
Much that was Scottish you might trace
In every feature of his face :
The full dark eye, so deeply set,
Bespoke him what is seldom met—
Intelligent, and true, and brave ;
The lips, determined, stern, and grave,
Save, when he smiled, that smile reveal'd
Much that was oftener far concealed,
A spring of hidden tenderness,
A wealth of feeling few could guess.
It won him trusting sympathy
From hearts of innocence and glee ;
While those to whom he best was known,
Ever most readily would own,
To gain his heart was worth endeavour—
If once a friend, a friend for ever.
By doubt or danger uneffaced,
Even in his sternest moods was placed,
On brow, and lips, and in his eye,
The seal of changeless constancy.
More pleasantly the time to pass,
He took his sketch-book from the grass,

But often stopped to fondly view,
The picture that his pencil drew ;
So fascinating had it grown,
He saw naught else but it alone,
Till Esther sprang from 'neath the trees,
Swinging her bonnet in the breeze ;
But quickly then the book was shut,
And lightly flung into the boat ;
While Donald hastened to her side,
With looks that would not be denied,
This once, expression of the love
That ever in his bosom strove
For freedom to reveal its tale
Of earnest truth.　'T were no avail,
For Donald knew 't was unreturned,—
If told, 't would be but to be scorned.

He spoke the common words of greeting
In accents low, his strong heart beating
With hopes that words could scarce convey,
That pleasantly might pass the day, —
A prelude to a year more bright
Than e'er had dawned on mortal sight ;
And that she might be spared to see
Many an anniversary ;
Circled by tenderness and truth,
And all the friends she loved in youth.

Gently he placed her in the boat,
And took the oars to row it out
Of the small creek in which it lay,
And down the lake, two miles away.

At first each seemed to like the best
Gaily to talk, and laugh, and jest;
At first, it was not very long,
Till talking was exchanged for song.
The human voice has never found
A rival in the realm of sound.
And now (with Donald's deeper tone,
Mingling and strengthening their own)
Sweetly the girls' young voices fall,
In accents clear and musical;
The very birds would stop to try
And catch the simple melody,
That far excelled the warbled notes
Which issued from their tiny throats.
But as they near'd the land again,
The happy singers ceased their strain.

On shore, they quickly bent their course,
To view the fall of Aira Force.
'T was strange, that knowing fears so few,
Brought up amongst the mountains, too,
Esther should always trembling dread,
Near chasm, or ravine to tread;

So giddy, she could scarcely stand,
But trusted now to Donald's hand
To guide her down the rocky pass,
And cross the torrent at its base.
There, he would not the hand release
He held so fondly clasped in his,
Till on it he had pressed a kiss.
Esther was puzzled to rebuke
The liberty her guardian took;
Glancing up quickly in his face,
Nought but amusement she could trace,—
None of the tenderness she sought.
Too clearly he perceiv'd her thought;
A look so unconcern'd as his
Could follow but a brother's kiss.
He gaily met her glance and smiled,
Treating her as but still a child;
And so the act pass'd unreproved,
Though much resented, half approved;
Th' interpretation fond and true
From woman's instinct Esther knew;
More dear than sister she was prized,
And love can rarely be disguised,
Whenever in the heart it dwells,
Its presence there—strange magic—tells.

All who 've seen Aira's waters falling,
When to their memory recalling,

The solemn awe that o'er them stole
While listening to their angry roll,
Know something of the mystic spell
That on their buoyant spirits fell,
As Donald Ross and Esther stood,
To watch the swift descending flood
Pour itself down, in raging heat,
To the abyss beneath their feet.
To them it imaged solemnly
Time rushing towards eternity!
Silent and awed, they bent their gaze
On what they held too high for praise,
Till Jessie's merry voice again
Broke on the stillness of the glen,
Calling them from the narrow bridge,
Resting on rock and mountain ridge,
Above the fall, to join her there,
Following her up the rocky stair—
And view its glories from the height.
Declaring 't was a glorious sight.
There, Esther terrified, and pale,
Rehearsed the legendary tale
Of Emma and Sir Eglamore,
And did her tragic fate deplore;
Then much they talked of scenes more grand.
In Scotland and in Switzerland.
And, passing from their mountain stream,
They dwelt on many a distant theme;

People and manners, lands and books,
Were all discussed with kindling looks;
Strange tales of cities he had seen,
And foreign shores on which he 'd been,
Of lands remote, yet highly famed,
The curious girls from Donald claimed;—
Till forced by time to leave the spot,
And wend their way back to the boat.

Chiding the loiterers' delay,
And wondering much what caused their stay—
Fearful lest ill should Esther reach,
Her anxious father sought the beach,
Just as the trio drew to shore,
And Donald laid aside his oar,
To lend the merry maids his aid,
As to the ground their leap they made.
Now Mr. Stafford claimed the right
Himself to help them to alight,
And Jessie first gallantly kissed,—
She hardly caring to resist,—
Then clasp'd his daughter to his breast,
Tenderly fondled her and blessed.
As towards the hall they sauntered on,
His glance fell ever and anon,
Proudly upon his darling child;
By her his thoughts seemed all beguiled.

His nature was a kindly one,
With much of good in it to atone
For want of strength in mind and will,
Too pliant far, yet graceful still ;
Like twining plant, that gropes its way
Till it can find some surer stay
Than its own stem, so weak and frail,
That yields to every passing gale ;
Yet its dependence seems to be
A fair and graceful thing to see,
Till its short summer-time soon past,
It fades the first in winter's blast,
And stripp'd of all the leaves and flowers
That had adorn'd its youthful hours,
When cultured and admired and prized,
In its old age 't is oft despised ;
Yet, even then, the boughs extend
Themselves in sweeping curves, and bend,
Light and elastic still, forsooth,
As in the sunshine of their youth.

The party soon arrived at home,
And Esther sought her mother's room ;
For, though the morning meal was laid,
Secluded there the lady stayed,
Waiting till their return should call
For her to join them in the hall.

C

Reclining on a sofa, now,
Gentle and peaceful was her brow;
Yet suffering's signet rested there,
And marks of sorrow and of care.
Strange contrast 't was, as Esther knelt,
And on her bright young forehead felt
That mother's kiss, so pure and mild,
And heard the prayer, ' God bless my child! '
The one seemed more akin to heaven,
As though its holy joys were given,
Her every thought and hope to engage,
And cheer her on her pilgrimage;
The other, a glad child of earth,
Holding its trifles things of worth,
Her face its noblest beauty wore,
To heaven's alone inferior;
And even that, reflected, shone
As reverently she gazed upon
Her mother's calm and placid face,
And heard her tell of Jesu's grace,
And humbly hope her child might prove
The tender shielding of His love,
Till with her Lord she should sit down,
And wear for aye the victor's crown.

The boudoir where the ladies sat,
Enlivening work with friendly chat,
Through the warm hours of cheerful morn,
Had doors that open'd on the lawn,

And through them stole into the room
Nature's sweet sounds, and rich perfume
Of flowers that gemm'd the garden beds,
And raised their many-colour'd heads
To catch the soft reviving breeze,
That rustled shily through the trees.
Idling in cushion'd easy chair,
With comfort's most luxuriant air,
Esther was weaving silken thread
In garlands gay on canvas spread ;
But 't was not much the work advanced,
So temptingly before her danced
The sunbeams on each object thrown,
That she was fain to put it down
And revel in those dear delights
To which earth's beauty oft invites.

But once, at dusk, had Jessie been
The neighbouring town of Penrith in,
When Donald brought her from the north.
Now thither he had ridden forth,
With Mr. Stafford, to attend
A meeting that had been convened,
Some public matters to discuss;
And in his absence Jessie chose
To learn from Esther what she knew
Both of the town and people too.
It was not much she could relate,
Her tales were more of ancient date :

But she described the beacon wood,
Where Cromwell's soldiery had stood
Upon the castle walls to fire,—
That fortress now a ruin dire
Of shattered fragments, crumbling fast,
Trembled and bent with every blast;
She told how dwellings circled round
The gloomy church, and churchyard ground,
And, 'tomb'd within the last, did sleep,
With six large stones his grave to keep,
A giant, dreaded far and wide
By the whole town and country side;
For every beauteous maiden near,
He captured, and removed to drear
Imprisonment within his caves,
Upon the banks that Eamont laves.
Till, one day, a young damsel strained
Her wits and nerves, and freedom gained.
Once having reached the open air
She had no time to dally there,
But, in the hurry of her flight,
Mistook the path, turned to the right,
And ran along the narrow ledge
Of rock, above the river's edge,
Unmindful of the depths below,
Of rocks above as heedless too;
But very soon her steps were stayed,
And sorely was the girl dismay'd,

To find the path o'er which she went,
For near five feet apart was rent.
In terror on the sight she gazed;
The farther side was slightly raised,
While, swollen by a recent flood,
Down yards below the river flowed.
She might not pause awhile to think,
For, as she stood upon the brink,
The giant in pursuit she heard,
Muttering full many an angry word,
With awful threats of vengeance rife.
To her, escape was more than life ;
So, venturing one desperate bound,
She safely cleared the space, and found
Herself upon the other side ;
Then ran, as though she 'd have defied
Even her tyrant's rapid stride .
To overtake her footsteps fleet,
Or hinder her abrupt retreat.
The giant's frame with fury shook
As he beheld the leap she took :
There he had deemed his prize secure ;
Now he must speed to make it sure.
For him to pass across the gap,
Was but an ordinary step;
But, in his blinding rage and haste,
His foot unevenly he placed,
And stumbling, headlong swift was hurl'd,
And lifeless down the stream was whirl'd.

The peasants still in memory keep
The story of ' The Maiden's Leap,'
And show the spot and tell the tale
To strangers visiting their vale ;
And should some sceptic doubt the force
Of Eamont's gentle gurgling course
To take away a giant's breath,
Though bruised and wounded unto death,
Or bear him onward in its flow,
Still nearer to the town below,
They 'd tell of frequent fearful floods,
And loss of life, and loss of goods,
And point him to a church that stands
Close by upon the level lands
The other side the stream, and say,
How eight times it was washed away —
The sacred edifice laid low
Each time by Eamont's overflow ;
A ninth rebuilt, received the name
Of Nine-Churches, to tell its fame ;
Of such convincing proofs apprised,
Right heartily would be despised
All those who might refuse to hold
As truth, past doubt, the tale they told.

Though Esther was as wild and free
As light wind sweeping o'er the lea,
Her mind had been improved with care,
And to its natural powers—as rare

As they were good and excellent—
Was added to a great extent
The light that erudition lends
To him who as her votary bends.
Well tutor'd by the clergyman
Of the next hamlet she had been—
A man bereft of child and wife,
Leading a lonely, studious life,
Secluded from the world without,
His sole companions books and thought :
Yet, in his youth he had been thrown
'Mongst men of note, and much had known
Of active life and busy ways,
And mixed therein in other days,
Which gave the converse of his age
That sprightly charm, so sure to engage
And captivate the gay and young,
Like minstrel tune that 's sweetly sung.
The mere book-drudge may toil in vain
The same extent of power to gain,
While God has given him eyes to see
His wondrous works by land and sea,
And in the starry heavens above.
Shutting them out, he 'd rather prove
Their beauties from the words of men,
At second-hand, then praise again.
But little can such praises move
The sympathies, or wake the love,

Of young hearts still to nature true,
And wrapp'd in spring-time's rosy hue.
Such rich reward is not for him
Presumingly to hope to claim.
Nature ne'er spoke to him a word,
Nor may he touch one single chord
Within the breasts that own her reign,—
Unmoved and silent they 'd remain.

A different man was Cyril Grey,
Easy to love as to obey,
His generous and tender heart
Claim'd as its own no trivial part
In joys or sorrows that befel
The people of his charge ; and well
He knew how to console the sad,
Or trace the blessings of the glad
Back to the Source of every good,
Urging the while their gratitude.
Less as a tutor he appeared
To Esther than as friend revered ;
Though he had sought her mind to store
With ancient and with modern lore,
Teaching her much for many a year
Of properties of earth and air,
Planets that roll in distant space,
Rocks, rivers, seas, that find a place
Upon the surface of the earth ;
And of the country of her birth ;

She learned of many a mighty state,
Its rapid rise and downfall great—
Of men who won a weighty name,
As wise, or valorous, known to fame ;
And languages the ancients used,
With some o'er Europe then diffused ;
Well versed, too, was she in the classics,
Nor all unknown were mathematics.
In later times she 'd been a ' blue ; '
Much more, when knowledge, shared by few,
Gained its possessors vast renown,
And wreath'd for them a laurel crown.
Yet all unconscious was the maid
Of homage to her talents paid :
If compliments they won, she smiled
As artless as a very child.

To greet her on her natal day,
And wish her well, came Cyril Grey.
The girls were busy with their flowers,
Whiling away the pleasant hours,
Nor once perceived their visitor
Till Wallace, who was standing near,
With loving zeal himself addressed
To give a welcome to their guest.
A favour'd guest, not hard to spy
From the bright light in Esther's eye,

As, turning round to where he stood,
Her dear and aged friend she viewed.
His presence brought them no restraint —
They laughed and talked without constraint ;
And, joining in their youthful glee,
None laughed more merrily than he.
At length, at Esther's strong desire,
He read (till Donald and her sire
Return'd) a short and simple lay—
The newest lyric of the day :
The maidens, placed on either side,
Industriously their needles plied,
While grassy bank for seats was tried.
Eagerly listening to the rhyme,
Unheeded, slipped away the time,
Till Donald's voice first broke the spell,
Wond'ring what book could charm so well.

The news was quickly ask'd and told,
For to their quiet mountain hold,
If news e'er came, it travelled slow,
In some chance tossing to and fro.
Few visits to the town were paid ;
But, when were such excursions made,
What they had heard and seen, to say
Occupied near a summer's day ;

Their purchases were held to be
A sort of general property,
And books and papers ransack'd o'er,
For weeks to come a precious store.

A fine old picture Donald brought—
A ship at sea, with perils fraught,
For fearfully the waters raged—
And as they looked a war was waged,
Of merry words, as to the theme,
Best suited for an artist's dream.
Most beauty Mr. Stafford found
In stately stag, or noble hound ;
While the old pastor better loved
A simple landscape, far removed
From 'strife, or passion, where peace reigned :
And Esther sturdily maintain'd,
'T was far the pleasantest to trace
The outlines of a human face,
Employing both the hand and head,
For, as the fingers o'er it sped,
Fancy would weave its history,
Winning the drawer's sympathy,
Till it almost a friend became,
And had a pictured home and name.
' Not less, my child,' said Cyril Grey,
' Need thought entwine itself, and play

Among scenes scattered all abroad,
' From Nature up to Nature's God,—'
Leading the soul, though that may be
Reflection more than reverie,
Yet dearer to a Christian heart
Than joys mere fancy can impart.'
Nothing was Esther's preference shook ;
But she confessed that each partook
A powerful charm to waken thought,
Yet held His living works were fraught
With marks of their Creator's hand,—
That equal homage should demand
From those to whom the grace was given,
That things of earth should speak of heaven.
Then, having yielded what he claimed,
A shaft was next at Donald aimed :
' I readily admit,' she said,
' Fitness of landscape or of head
To draw an artist's talents forth ;
Both time and labour they are worth ;
But who, in straight or curving lines
Of architectural designs,
Can find a beauty, or pretend
To hold communion with a friend ?
The noblest thoughts they can inspire,
Than human skill, can rise no higher,
Or seek perhaps to estimate
The cost of edifice so great.'

To Donald it was nought but fun
To hear her as she thus ran on,
Abusing what she knew to be
His work and pleasure equally;
But when her merry raillery ceased,
He strove to justify his taste,
And in the same light playful tone
Defended what he praised alone.
' But most I wonder,' he replied,
' You cannot imagery provide
For castle or cathedral stall ;
Or fancy ringing through the hall
The laugh of maid and warrior bold,
That echoed there in days of old ;
Or picture thousands gathering where
Arose the solemn voice of prayer ;
And hopes and fears that had a part
In many a throbbing lifted heart,
That long'd to feel devotion's calm,
Or for some sorrow sought a balm !
Sketches like these, it seems to me,
Not only boast utility,
But might inspire a poet's dream,
And were an artist's fittest theme.'

Esther was pleased he understood
The visionary dreams that glow'd

So brightly in her girlish breast,
And timidly she half confessed,
As Donald turn'd her folio o'er,
The character each drawing bore.
' That sailor boy, so blythe and gay, ⎤
With him I've travelled many a day, ⎬
In pleasant fancies far away ⎦
And stood beneath a tropic sun,
Or striven its glaring heat to shun,
By sheltering 'neath a feathery palm ;
Or watch'd, with terror and alarm,
The pagan rites of heathen lands,
In ignorance of Heaven's demands ;
Then sailing quickly towards the west,
Passing by shores in beauty dressed,
Gazed on those wondrous forests high,
That seem to mingle with the sky ;
Or view'd the prairie's vast extent,
Or watch'd the Indian in his tent ;—
Till with the seaman homeward bound,
Steering 'mong icebergs all around,
I've seen him smile with humid eye,
To think the happy hour was nigh,
When he would hear his father's voice,
And share his little sister's joys,
And feel once more his mother's kiss,
No home so dear, so blest as his.
So near, and yet it might not be,
The gallant ship was lost at sea,

And he so young, and glad, and brave,
Was buried in an ocean grave.
Yon aged prisoner, in his cell,
It seemed that I remember'd well;
When his grey hair was black as jet,
And he was good and true; and yet,
Once having yielded to the bait
Temptation held, his fall was great—
Great, but a thing of slow degrees,
Sin's chain at first was worn with ease,
For it was light; but, coil by coil,
It fastened closer on its spoil,
Till fetter'd, as by deadly grasp,
He might not free him from its clasp.
How sadly mourned his youthful wife,
That he she held more dear than life
Should alter thus; her fears at first
Mingled with hopes that trembling burst
From her still loving, trusting heart;
But soon, too soon, did hope depart,
And agony and dread despair
Poisoned a flower that bloom'd so fair.
But this bright child was happier theme,
Smiling at some pure baby dream,
As though in sleep he seemed to hear
The angels whisper in his ear;
While o'er his couch his mother bends,
And lovingly her darling tends.

But, Donald, now I claim from you
Sight of a sketch and story, too:
The one your thoughts so much beguiled
This morning, for I saw you smiled.'
A curious light shone in his eye,
At loss he seemed for some reply—
Half hesitating to obey   )
The mandate of the maiden gay ;   }
Yet scarcely venturing to say, 'nay.'   )
But hesitation soon gave place
To his accustomed easy grace ;
And, with a mirthful glance that bode
Some hidden mischief, proudly show'd
A likeness of her own fair face—
So like, she could not fail to trace
Her image there.   Her blush and start
Show'd it was recognised : apart
The rest had drawn some time before,
And Donald, lightly bending o'er
Her shoulder, ask'd if he should tell
Musings that he had loved so well.
She gave a deprecating look,
While mortified to feel how shook
Her hand and voice beneath his eye—
Nor could she guess the reason why ;
But, such unwonted change to hide,
Assumed an air of injured pride ;
Then, finding night was drawing on,
Wonder'd where Jessie could be gone,

And went to seek her to prepare,
The evening's festive mirth to share,
And Donald, cold and proud as she,
Wander'd the gardens solemnly.

Can English hearts be growing cold,
That now 'tis thought a fashion old,
Unfit for stirring times like these,
When bustling haste seems best to please,
To welcome birthdays as they fall
With kindly words and smiles from all,
That tender ties of kindred bind,
Whose hearts are fondly intertwined?
Not mine a foolish vain desire,
That pomp and worldly show conspire
The joys such days should bring to prove.
But rather that the voice of love
With thankfulness should hail the hour
That gave a dear and treasured flower,
(In years gone by) so fragrantly
To bloom beneath the household tree.
The child that feels his parents' kiss,
While from their tender hearts to his
Comes the assurance, loved the best,
They hold that hour as doubly blest
Which gave to them a child so dear,
A child they pray that God may spare,

D

Longs with strange yearning still to be
Their joy and comfort; bitterly
He mourns that e'er he gave them pain,
And vows to do so ne'er again.
Brothers and sisters smiling come,
To greet the sharer of their home,
So pleased, so kind, he thinks it strange
That ever he could interchange
With them one angry word or look,
And hopes thenceforth to meekly brook
Some little petulance of will,
Since each so dearly loves him still.
'Tis true that love awakens love,
And those who wish at home to prove
Affection's joys will surely find
A little word or action kind,
Or fond caress, like magic, smooth
Tempers' unevenness, and soothe
The spirits care has fretted sore;
O'er all love reigns a conqueror.
Many will doggedly admit,
For youth or homes of gladness fit
The pleasant look or gentle tone,
But all unsuited to their own
Dark moods of care, or sorrow stern ;
Love should depart till joy's return.
Oh ! that they would but bid it stay
To cheer and comfort while it may,

While long to them remains unknown
Life's bitterest grief, to weep alone.

Brightly the day on Esther beam'd,
From every eye she met there gleamed
The light of love, so gladsomely,
Her young heart overflow'd with glee;
Of all she saw the hope and pride,
Oh! who would too severely chide,
If nestling deep within her breast,
Unworthier feelings sought to rest?
For she was but of mortal birth,
And kindred claim'd with things of earth.
And oft, too oft, will self intrude
E'en on the musings of the good,
By age, or sorrow, taught to know
The vanity of all below.
To give to joy still livelier tone,
Nor share it by themselves alone,
Her sire had bidden many a guest,
To join the social evening feast
He held in honour of his child,
And brightly she and Jessie smiled,
As with unwonted care they sought
To choose the vestments that they thought
Would best befit a scene so gay;
And never has the light of day

On fairer forms, or happier hearts,
Than those young maidens', flung his darts,
While vainly they call'd art to aid
The charms that nature had displayed,
Such thoughts in Donald's mind arose,
When presently again they chose
To join him (for the hour grew late),
The coming of their friends to wait;
And Esther's face with kindness glowed,
Nor trace of her resentment show'd.
The flickering firelight on them fell,
And Donald played the watcher well,
Till, yielding to some sudden thought,
He hastily the greenhouse sought,
But soon again at Esther's side
Displayed the skill with which he'd tried
For each a floral wreath to twine,
Among their lovely locks to shine.
Of lilies of the vale was made
The one designed for Jessie's head,
While that which Esther's brow should grace
(And Donald there himself would place)
Was of the plant her name expressed,
Of love's sure token held possessed;
Sacred to Esther and to Love,
The myrtle flowers of which he wove
The tiny wreath, to Donald seemed,
And bright as stars of hope they gleamed,

When he had twined them in her hair,
And she, consenting, deign'd to wear;
But other guests soon claimed the right
To hail her of the festive night
The honoured queen, for many strove
To win her favour or her love,
And young hearts far and near had felt
The passion that in Donald's dwelt;
But hers was all unruffled still,
Ever obedient to her will,
Nor did she give one treacherous smile,
To deeper bondage to beguile
Those who her power so freely own'd;
But guardedly on all she frowned
(Save Donald), if they dared to show
The hopes that smouldered deep below
The outward surface, and to him
Often indifferent she would seem,
When the best dictates of her heart
Taught her to act a truthful part;
But sometimes (chafed, he could repress
So easily what none the less
He felt for her of strong regard)
She strove by hope of sure reward
Falsely to lure him to her feet,
And make her triumphing complete.
Joyously passed that birthday eve,
With nought to dread and nought to grieve,

For every sparkling eye was bright,
And every heart was fluttering light,
And full content, and game, and song
Hurried the rapid hours along,
Until the breaking of the dawn
Announced the early hours of morn,
And chariot after chariot bore
Visitors quickly from the door.
Soon all were gone, each vacant room
Seem'd wrapt in silence and in gloom,
And quench'd were all the brilliant lights,
While interchanging fond ' Good nights ';
Their chambers soon the Staffords sought ;
But still with Esther's dreamy thought
Music and laughter seem'd to blend,
And slumber long refused to lend
Refreshment to her weary eyes,
For ever and anon would rise
Before her visions of the day,
To chase all hope of sleep away ;
Yet stealing over her at last,
In close embrace it locked her fast.
Childlike and peaceful was her rest,
Her lot with every blessing blest.

PART SECOND.

Has Earth one single tranquil spot
Of which to say, it changes not?
Ever from year to year the same,
Well might it bear a world-wide fame!
Or when her myriad voices speak
Of alter'd scenes or fortune's freak,
Could one through ign'rance fail to tell
A tale the others knew so well?
Beats there a human heart that ne'er
Has known alternate hope and fear,
Joy chasing sorrow, sorrow joy,
Good seeking evil to destroy,
All striving to possess the ground,
And each in turn the conqueror found?
There is not one; 'tis passing strange,
All that is earthly speaks of change;
However fair, however good,
The mark of stern vicissitude
Rests upon each material form—
All prove alike both calm and storm;
The flower that freshly blooms to-day
To-morrow will be swept away;
First draped with foliage, then with snow,
For centuries the oak may show

Defiance to each angry blast,
But it must surely fall at last ;
The rill that ripples o'er the ground
Will soon by frost-chain tight be bound,
And shifting sands, now here, now there,
Are blown by every breath of air ;
The billows on the ocean's breast,
Heaving and tossing, ne'er at rest,
Join in the loud tumultuous roar,
Then softly sighing touch the shore ;
And although mortal life is short,
With strange experience it is fraught,
Of struggling hope and yielding fear,
Calm fortitude and sad despair ;
For one brief moment joy's sweet song
May echo gladly from the tongue,
But ere the strain has ceased to flow
It turns again to notes of woe.
Mirror'd upon the silent sky,
Say, does not Earth's reflection lie
Of constant change ? We seldom view
It one vast canopy of blue ;
A thousand fleecy clouds of light,
Flitting and hurrying out of sight,
Spread themselves over it awhile,
Then, heap'd in one tremendous pile,
They gather blackness, and essay
To intercept the light of day,
Imprisoning each sunlit ray ;

Perchance a sheet of leaden hue
Obscures the faintest tint of blue,
Anon, dissolving into tears,
It melts away and disappears.
Riding triumphant o'er the plains,
With pride surveying his domains,
The dazzling sun we oft behold,
Mid clouds of purple and of gold;
But presently he sinks to rest,
And gorgeous crimson paints the west,
Like some grand monarch by his train
Close follow'd o'er a distant plain.
The glorious pageant soon sweeps by,
A few faint streaks like stragglers lie,
But one by one they fade from sight,
We look again, and lo! 't is night.
For ever varying, ne'er the same,
The farthest limits change will claim
Of its vast territory; high
It writes itself upon the sky,
But there it finds its utmost bound,
It may not, cannot pass beyond
Where dwells th' Almighty Changeless One,
And stands secure th' Eternal Throne.

One little year had slipt away,
And dark and dense the shadows lay

On Stafford Hall; no more was heard
The merry laugh or playful word;
For death had silenced accents sweet,
And fetter'd hearts that used to beat
With tenderness for her whose fate
Was now so sad and desolate.
Esther was orphan'd ; fell the stroke
That first upon her gladness broke,
When a few months before was borne
Homeward, one long-remember'd morn,
With solemn awe and heavy tread,
Her father's corpse, for he was dead !
Early that day he left his home,
With an old sporting friend to roam
Across the moors, and try what skill
They might possess at shooting still;
And as they went he laughed, and told
Frolics and jests they shared of old,
Till grown excited by his theme,
And walking half as in a dream,
He fell upon the slippery turf;
At once his loaded gun went off,
Lodging its contents in his side,
And without word or sign he died !
Sadly his daughter learned the truth,
It crush'd the freshness of her youth ;
Sitting at work, with much surprise
She followed those, with curious eyes,

Who with his lifeless body came,
Amazed to think that house their aim ;
She watched them halt awhile and wait,
Speaking in whispers, at the gate,
Then enter ; dread of unknown ill,
Forebodings that she could not still,
Crept to her heart and blanched her cheek ;
Breathless, without the power to speak.
She hurried forth with flying feet,
The slow advancing train to meet :
She saw with undefined alarm
The outline of a human form,
Beneath the covering concealed,—
To her the truth it half revealed ;
Closer she pressed ; none bade her stay,
None sought to draw her thence away,
Not one to break the tidings tried,
But, panic-struck, they stepp'd aside,
And suffer'd her to lift the pall ;
Alas ! poor child, she saw it all !
Saw it with conscious agony ;
Her limbs seemed failing, and her eye
Riveted by that ghastly face,
As though she could not choose but gaze
No tear-drop came, but pale and cold
She stood and listened while they told
How it had happened, when and where,
Then bade them follow up the stair

The servants used; all sound to keep
From breaking on her mother's sleep ;
For hers was now the settled doom
Of invalids, and in her room
She sought from pain some slight relief
In soothing sleep, however brief.

Now soon her slumber must be broken,
And the sad truth be gently spoken ;
But who, oh ! who, to her could dare
Tidings so terrible to bear ?
Poor Esther knew not whom to ask
To undertake the dreaded task ;
No one was there she could entrust ;
The work was hers, she felt she must
Brace every nerve, and calmly strive
From her wrung heart each thought to drive
Of self and sorrow, and prepare
Her mother's grief to soothe and share.
' Twere better she should know at once ;
So, with the sad intelligence,
Her daughter slowly sought her side,
Struggling the gushing tears to hide,
That now so swift and freely came
Whene'er she spoke her father's name.
But let the closing chamber door
Hide from our view the grief that tore
The widow'd heart when stricken sore
Beneath the overwhelming stroke

Esther herself so gently broke.
When others saw her she appear'd
Strangely composed, but much they feared,
As day by day her chasten'd brow
Shone with more peaceful, saintlike glow,
The blow severe her soul had riven ;
Soon Earth would have to yield to Heaven
The purest heart that beat within
Precincts so much defiled by sin.
Time proved the doubt was sadly true;
Hourly she faded from their view ;
The sands of life were nearly run,
Its brittle thread was almost spun,
For fast the closing hours had sped,
When gather'd round her dying bed
Were the old pastor and her child,
With Jessie Ross ;—on each she smiled,
And whispering words of love and faith,
Entered the dark, dark stream of death.
Deep were its waters, but it seemed
As though above her brightly beam'd
Some face she long had loved and known,
That never ceased to cheer her on,
Uphold, and guide her through the haze
Of doubt and danger, for her gaze
Steadfastly ever upward turned,
And as she looked her mild eyes burned
With strange, mysterious light, as though
Reflected glory, shining so,

Revealed itself to others near,
Who might not feel, or see, or hear
What to the dying saint was clear;
Clearer than earthly sight or sound,
Save one, when fondly glancing round,
To comfort Esther's grief she strove,
With fond unutterable love,
Strove with her failing, voiceless breath,
Till it was sealed at length in death.

Three months had passed since that sad day,
And Esther now, no longer gay,
Sat lonely at that evening hour
When every spire and tree and tower
Stands forth with a distincter form,
And the blue sky, untouched by storm,
Or lower'd by intervening cloud
That seeks its loftiness to shroud,
Appears to rise in boundless space,
And take a more majestic place,—
Lonely she sat and watched the scene,
But not of it her thoughts I ween;
For as she looked the tears would start,
And sighs escape her troubled heart,
Till by her will's controlling force
She resolutely checked their course,
And turning to her work again,
Strove hard her sorrow to restrain.

Life's hopes and joys had changed no more
Than she from what she was of yore;
The merry playful child had fled,
And rising graceful in its stead
The woman moved and spoke and thought,
And energetic calmness fraught
The face so late with bliss endued,
For grief had saddened, not subdued;
Pride linger'd still within her breast,
More as a monarch than a guest,
Not now by sudden flash displayed,
That every angry thought obeyed,
But changeless dignity, so stern,
So cold, so still, one seemed to yearn
To see such icy hauteur shook
By one spontaneous childlike look.
Sorrow and pride! they should not meet,
Their union renders woe complete.
The same sweet hour saw swiftly rowing,
Against the breezes lightly blowing,
Over the lake a tiny skiff;
To guide it was a task so stiff,
It needed Donald's utmost strength
To land it in the creek at length.
He sat alone; the freshening gale
Seemed welcome, for his cheek was pale,
Almost as though he had been vexed,
Or troubled, or was sore perplexed;

His brow uncover'd, it appeared
As though the toil the task endeared,
For strange and wayward was his mood,
Work was its need, for work it sued;
But calmer soon, he drew to shore,
Still in the boat he poised his oar,
Then let it in the water dip,
But raised it up to watch the drip
Of liquid beads, as one by one
They sought observant eyes to shun,
Till mingling with their native deep,
They sank again in peaceful sleep.
Blending with that low trickling sound,
Donald for his excitement found
A vent in mournful wish and plaint,
Though both were uttered soft and faint:
' I dared not hope to call her wife,
But I did trust to spend my life
Where every day I might rejoice
To listen to her girlish voice,
And gaze upon her sweet young face,
So sad now in its loveliness,
To sorrow near her when she wept,
And tread the ground o'er which she stepped,
To clasp her little hand in mine,
For one brief moment, nor resign
The intercourse a *friend* might claim,
For mine, I hold that sacred name;

And if at times in day dreams, fleet
As they were false, but passing sweet,
I won the prize for which I strove,
And years, long years, of patient love
Gain'd love in sweet return at last,
Why should such dreams so soon be past?
Now all is changed ! and though they say
Still in her childhood's home she 'll stay,
My own heart tells me 't is not true ;
Hers, when she learns the truth, will sue
For change of scene, should choice be left ;
But much I fear, of home bereft,
Necessity may urge her forth,
And far, far distant from the North,
Toil and unkindness be her fate,
In poverty's enslaving state.
'T is hard to think that I, aloof,
May never know the sheltering roof
'Neath which is all she finds of home,
But only in the sky's blue dome,
So wide and lofty, recognize
Her certain tent ; for that defies
Time's utmost efforts to eject
From its cold shielding those who 've wreck'd
Fortune, or better home, or friends ;
Ever o'er all alike it bends—
On happy child and wretch forlorn,
By life of sin and sorrow worn,

Light from Heaven's radiant lamps will fall,—
It spreads its covering over all.
My suffering seems hard ; but worse,
A hundredfold, to think of hers,—
Her young heart breaking all alone,
Beneath the world's unkindly frown.
It must not, will not, shall not be ;
Esther, I cannot part from thee !'
He clasped his hands in anguish dread,
And silently he bow'd his head ;
But when again he raised it up
It glowed with a determined hope ;
Again his voice the silence broke,
And firmly hope and purpose spoke,
' Love so intense and strong as mine
Must be successful ; I resign
A chance of bliss for certain woe ;
Without an effort I forego
Happiness that I might obtain ;
My suit might not be all in vain :
Perhaps she only tried to spare
Encouragement, my love to dare
Its strength to tenderly avow ;
Right earnestly I'll plead it now,
And may success attend my cause !
To weigh results I dare not pause.
Would I could find some hidden spell,
To win the heart I prize so well !

Tenderest devotion should repay
The priceless gift from day to day.
I 'll plead to night, before she hears
That she is poor, and proudly fears
Some may adopt the grovelling thought
That conquest love could ne'er have wrought
Was gained by offer of a home,
Humble and mean, if spared to roam
'Mid scenes of hardship and distress.
Her answer then I well could guess—
Love whom she might, however long
Or truthfully, both hearts she 'd wrong,
Poor child ! before she 'd dare to brave
The world's false censure.   If I crave
Acceptance now it may be given ;
Morning would every hope have riven.'
When once resolved he did not wait,
Nor heeded that the hour grew late,
But hastened to the maiden's side ;
Though harrowing doubts he strove to hide,
Even from himself, his heart oppressed
And forced their power to be confessed.

Indifferent greeting Esther gave,
Relapsing soon to silence grave,
Till Donald's tale of love bespoke
Her heart's attention, and awoke

A trembling, strange, responsive thrill,
That pride itself could scarcely still.
With all a child's simplicity,
A man's deep, fervent energy,
He told the secret of his breast,—
Love, hope, and fear were all confest,
And she was asked to be his wife,
Accept his love, and share his life.
He did not ask the same degree
Of earnest tenderness that he
In his wild passion had bestowed;
If in her heart but faintly glowed
Affection's fire, 't was almost more
Than he had dared to hope before,—
Confiding love (though cold and calm),
The right to shield her safe from harm,
Was all he sought.   His pleading eye
Urged more than words for kind reply.
Esther was gratified to hear
By Donald she was held so dear;
His best beloved, most precious one,
She did not feel so quite alone :
Her heart, acknowledging his power,
Saw dreamily some future hour,
When she might graciously afford
To give the coveted reward ;
Not now,—he must not think so soon,
So easily, her heart was won ;

'Twas right he should endure suspense,
And grieve at her indifference;
And if reproachful words she spoke,
That torture in his bosom woke,
As if led on by spirit ill,
That seemed a greater triumph still;
And so she spoke them, though she knew
The doubts implied were all untrue;
Regard for Donald had been small,
When self-love overcame it all.
Thus she began, in freezing tone,
'Donald, I am surprised, I own,
That such a subject you should choose
At such a time to introduce,
When scarcely three short months have passed
Since death deprived me of the last
Dear friend I had; yet you would dare
Attempt their memory's shrine to share!
Real affection had concealed
Its own existence, or revealed
Itself in sympathy alone,
Not irksome and demanding grown.
And more, such words were ne'er addressed,
Nor did you venture such request,
To me while yet my father lived,
And pardon me if I believed,
I think not wrongly, that his land
Lent value to his daughter's hand.

Soon as the one the other brought
With earnest diligence 't was sought ;
Not long ago you had not cared
To slight and scorn it, had you dared.'

Amazed at first had Donald heard
Distinctly each disdainful word.
The purport soon of her reply,
He understood ; indignantly
His nature spurn'd repulse so base,—
Such insult nothing could efface ;
To her who could so far forget
His honour, and his truth, not yet
An answer dared he to return,
Lest stern contempt and raging scorn
Should utter in a lady's ear
What, though he felt, she might not hear.
How could he e'er for her have felt
Pure fervent love, like that which dwelt
So late within his heart? Ashamed,
The weakness of the past he blamed :
Never again such love should rise
For one he only could despise.
What if he cleared himself, forsooth,
And proudly flinging back the truth,
Left her to be consoled by pride,
That courtesy and truth denied.

Strange comforter ! Nay, Donald, nay,
Despise yourself as weak you may ;
But you must love her. With the thought
Rush'd back the feeling that he sought ,
To crush for ever from his heart ;
With life alone would it depart.
He gazed upon her figure, slight
And small, drawn to its utmost height,
Her curling lip and stately mien,
And never dearer had she been.
The angry fire forsook his eye,
And, sinking into pity's sigh,
His voice, in accents calm and sad,
A half reproachful answer made.
'Esther ! you wrong me, for you know
That I could never stoop so low ;
My love I had not dared to tell,
But none the less you knew it well,
Knew that I loved yourself alone,—
That every look for years had shown.
Some time perhaps you may believe
It was too truthful to deceive ;
You spurn it, but it does not die,
It lives in fervent constancy ;
Time every other friend may change,
My love it never can estrange,
Your weal will be my life-long prayer,
My constant thought, my hope, my care ;

And should you ever want a friend,
Help in a trying hour to lend,
Somewhat to ease my heavy cross,
Promise to think of Donald Ross.
Farewell.' He sought her hand to clasp
In one last, lingering, parting grasp;
But haughtily it was withdrawn,
And loftily her head was borne,
Then, stepping back, she bow'd it low,
With most majestic air to show
Donald that now he was dismissed.
Her silent mandate to resist
He tried not, but inclined his head,
In answer to the move she made,
And left her with an aching breast,
Sad for himself, for her distressed.

Poor human nature is but weak,
Guided by many an idle freak,
Speaks what it would not wish to say,
And sorrows oft for many a day
O'er deeds deliberately done,
Though all the fruits such deeds had won
Clear in the distance had been viewed,
And eagerly and long pursued.
Scarcely had Donald closed the door
Than Esther, sobbing on the floor,

Heaped harsh reproaches on her head,
And vainly wish'd her words unsaid.
' Oh ! what could tempt me e'er to give
Utterance to doubts none could conceive
Of one so noble and so good,
Save meanest minds, with thoughts imbued
Loathsome and vile, and revelling
In wrong alone, attributing
To others motives of their own,
'Mid plots and schemes still crawling on ?
I am not quite like that, but still
Donald must think I am ; he will
Now spurn me as most mean and base,
Unworthy to have held a place
Within his heart ; and yet I cared
For his regard more than I dared
Ever even to myself confess—
Far more than he shall ever guess !
Vainly, but earnestly, I long,
Now, that I could repair the wrong ;
I only thought to rouse his ire,
And set his passions all on fire.
Truly I might have known full well
That Donald only would repel
Insult so gross with silence stern,—
Cold, calm contempt its sole return.
Not quite, for pity found a vent,
And gently with his sternness blent.

So sad, so hopeless, had he spoke
The thought that in his breast awoke,
Poor child ! had almost been the sound ;
But words in feeling all were drowned.
Some slight concession I would make,
And even his forgiveness take,
Rather than he should think I meant
Words that have degradation lent
To her who spake them ; in my heart
Such doubts had shared no real part.
An opportunity I'll seek,
Regret for what has passed to speak.'
And yet, had Donald then returned,
Although with heartfelt truth she yearned
For reconciliation, she
Had striven inconsistently
To gall with rudeness still more plain,
Inflicting yet a deeper pain.
Another friend the morrow brought,
With tidings of such strange import
To tell them he had scarcely dared,
For Cyril Grey had gladly spared
His pupil sorrow's lightest blow,
One single pang of grief; but now
His arm was powerless to avert
The stroke that threatened her with hurt.
Appointed by her father's will,
With Gerald Marsden, of the hill,

His joint executor, they deemed
Their duty light and easy seemed,
Till suddenly a claim was made
For payment of a debt delayed.
Long years ago, it seemed, he lost
Near all he had—a pricely cost—
For having sought one little while
With bets and gambling to beguile
A life of weary, listless ease,
Whose dissipation failed to please.
That mode of life was quickly done,—
Nothing but ruin had it won.
Quite at a loss what course to take,
Almost like light the thought did break
Across his mind, to mortgage all
His property, except the hall ;
That with the furniture left free,
All else was burdened heavily,
To gain enough with which to pay
His debts of honour—fruits of play.
One sole condition he imposed,—
The mortgage should not be foreclosed
During the period of his life,
Or that of his then youthful wife,
So long as interest, year by year,
Was given in payments regular.
His wife knew nothing of the deed,
She had known nothing of his need,

And for his child, it was his hope
Before his death to give her up,
As wife, to one whose joy should be
To cherish her right lovingly;
For vain had all his efforts proved,
Even for one so much beloved,
To save for what her wants might call,—
That yearly sum consumed it all.
Cyril explain'd, as best he might,
To his young ward their sudden plight;
The claim advanced they found too true,
From memoranda, brought to view
Since the disclosure, that her sire
Had kept, and an event so dire
Fully confirmed. The wisest course
('T was well he said things were not worse)
Would be to sell the mortgaged lands,
And when the creditor's demands
Were satisfied she might decide
Her future plans: the safest guide
Would be their failure or success
In well disposing of the place.
Six months the claimant would allow
To raise the sum, and when, and how,
The sale should be was left to them
To fix; their power alone to stem
Was the requirement to receive,
No less than he had dared to give,—

If the half year should pass away,
And they the mortgage fail'd to pay,
He then should claim the large estate
As his own property, nor wait,
Affording them a longer chance
Miss Stafford's interests to advance.

Paler at each successive word
Grew Esther's face ; composed she heard
Him tell the whole long story through,—
All it involved full well she knew.
One single fear had blanch'd her cheek,
And half denied her power to speak;
Yet speak she must, if but to gain
Assurance, added to the pain
Of doubt.   Her question she preferred,
Had Donald Ross or Jessie heard,
Or any other, how bereft
Of value the estate was left ?
Donald had heard, to him alone
The truth, in confidence, was known.
He had been told the day before ;
Responsibilities so sore
They scarcely dared to bear alone,
So ask'd him what had best be done.
He gave them what advice he could,
Though much abstracted seem'd his mood,

And urged for her the slight relief
Of respite for one evening brief
From knowledge harassing and strange,—
One evening free in thought to range,
Unfetter'd by the fact's stern truth,
Amid the gladsome hopes of youth.
On other things soon Cyril ran,
Suggesting many a minor plan
For their adoption.   Calm and still,
As though she feared no touch of ill,
While hearing, Esther understood,
Commented freely, and withstood
Various suggestions, or as great
Allow'd their wisdom and their weight.
He had to say 'Adieu' at length,
And physical and mental strength,
Exhausted by continued strain,
Now yielded to the aching pain
At Esther's heart : for once—but once—
His going seemed deliverance
From almost torture : she was free
To analyse her misery,—
Free for this once to give it vent.
Hereafter an assumed content
Must veil the wretched, weary woe
Her heart for long was doom'd to know.
By far the bitterest pang she felt
In mortified remembrance dwelt

Of her own vulgar, empty boast
Of wealth, to her for ever lost,
When Donald pleaded for her hand,
Insinuating that her land
Induced him the attempt to make.
Yet, knowing all, he did not take
Advantage of her, and with scorn
Proclaim her poverty forlorn.
' And why, oh why,' she sadly sigh'd,
' Should he have wished my loss to hide
From me that little while, and haste
Hither, before I saw the rest,
To tell a tale like his?   He might,
Surely he had, believed that night
Alone remained in which to prove
If he himself could win my love,
And that the morrow's grief might tempt
A feign'd return, that should exempt
From effort, that my helplessness
Would weakly shrink from in distress.
Better I had deserved his trust ; ⎫
A doubt like that was too unjust, ⎬
But bear it I suppose I must,— ⎭
Both must and will ; a pride like mine
Shall never by a word or sign
Succumb to sorrow, doubt, or slight,
Or wounded seem ; by its own might

It shall sustain itself and dare
To strive, to suffer, and to bear.'
Resolves were all awhile dispell'd,
As up the garden she beheld
Jessie, with lightsome step, advance.
Half shily she appeared to glance
Round for her friend, who to resume
Her wonted manner, and assume
A ladylike indifferent air,
Before she saw her, strove with care.
Just as 't was won a gentle hand
Drew back her face, and Jessie scann'd
It fondly, and, with warm caress,
Sought on her brow a kiss to press;
Then kneeling lightly by her side,
Her loving innocence defied
All Esther's wishes to repel
The sympathetic words that fell
From lips so youthful and so pure,
Striving to happier thoughts to lure.
Esther soon gathered that she knew
Nothing of Donald's interview,
As, all unconscious, did she grieve
That he had been obliged to leave
For London on that very morn,
Not knowing when he should return.
The rest she learned from Cyril Grey,
Who called, ere Donald left, to say

What calm and noble fortitude
Esther on hearing all had showed.
Then she descanted more at large
On Donald's grief; his parting charge
To join her friend, and strive to share
Her plans and sorrows, if she dare,
She soon disclosed; while Esther met
Her love with confidence, for yet
She scarcely could repulse bestow
On one like Jessie, or forego
The tenderness of such a friend,
Whose presence comfort seem'd to lend.
So at the hall for weeks she stayed,
Long as the sale could be delayed.

By private contract it was thought
For land the highest price was brought,
And so 't was tried ;—as time passed on
Of all their tenders only one
Was what they could accept, and it
The hall included ; but to quit
Its shelter Esther meant full soon.
They said if it were sold alone
A mere acknowledgment 't would gain :
The offered sum, though in the main
Far 'neath its value, yet would meet
Mortgage and each outstanding debt :

F

So 't was accepted; and, to raise
A tiny fund for rainy days,
All of the furniture was sold
By auction. Esther's heart grew cold
While, out of sight, she heard the stroke,
That oft upon the stillness broke,
Whene'er the hammer falling gave
Things that she had not power to save—
Familiar things her parents loved,
O'er which her childhood's eyes had roved—
For ever into strangers' hands,
No more to serve her own demands.

Dependent then for daily bread
Upon the efforts that she made,
A governess's life she chose :
She knew not half its stinging woes.
Her cultivated talents soon
A lucrative engagement won ;
But distant far she had to roam
From her own native mountain home.

Donald, with eager hurry, went
From London to the Continent,—
Anywhere, to prolong his stay.
Yet anxiously from day to day
Were Jessie's letters waited for ;
Tidings of all that passed they bore :

Esther's resolve the latest one
Told him, when fast he hastened on,
Homeward;—she never would deny
His right to claim a last ' Good bye.'
But letters then were oft delayed,
And Jessie's on the road had stayed
Too long for Donald to attain
The object that he hoped to gain.
He guessed not Esther was within
The little bustling Yorkshire inn
At which he waited for the coach
Going north; she, watching its approach
From out an upper window, viewed
Donald, in most impatient mood,
Enter, and quick they drove away ;—
Southward her own long journey lay.

Upon a small, low wicker chair
Jessie sat in the open air,
Attentive to the birds' sweet song,
Yet swift her needle sped along.
The cottage, and the beech and lake,
A livelier hue appeared to take,
As on them shone the full, warm sun,
That pierced each nook that afternoon;
Autumn with beauty tinged the trees,
But did not stir the faintest breeze.

Heated and tired, soon Jessie's eye
Over the lake roved longingly ;
But eager grew her listless glance,
As towards her she beheld advance
A little boat,—'t was Donald's hand,
She knew, that guided it to land.
Wallace (for he was left to share,
With Esther's linnet, Jessie's care)
Watch'd by her side, but soon a leap
He made, and through the water deep
Swam to the boat with loving haste,
To greet him, and to be caressed.
At home his sister soon explained
How the old favourite dog remained
With her, and much did she deplore
That Esther left two days before.
Donald a mere regret expressed ;
His deeper sorrow was repressed,
Till, lighted by the silvery moon,
He wander'd to the hall alone,
Visiting each deserted room,
While, echoing sadly through their gloom,
His footsteps seem'd a startling sound,
So hushed and still was all around.
Laid in the study, Donald saw,
'Mid paper waste and packing straw,
Something that like a drawing seemed,
And, as the moonbeams brightly gleamed

Upon it, gladly recognised
Esther's young sailor boy.   He prized
It more, far more, than words could tell—
It seemed a sort of magic spell,
Bringing her nearer; uneffaced,
Her name beneath he plainly traced.
The thought her hand had rested there,
And marked the characters so fair,
Was dear and soothing ; many a day
Impatient thoughts it charm'd away,—
A simple relic, treasured long,
Round which sweet memories used to throng.

PART THIRD.

THOSE natures own a blessed gift,
Endowed with power their sight to lift
Up to the sunshine and the skies,
While dark and dim their pathway lies;
Or glancing down upon the thorn
And rugged steep, the light of morn
That gilds them they alone perceive,—
Hopeless and crush'd, they cannot grieve!
Such was the bent of Esther's mind : ·
Beauty she never failed to find ;
And now her novel mode of life
Appear'd with many pleasures rife.
Her quiet dignity restrain'd
The slights that others might have pained.
Her pupils were two merry boys,
Whose romping glee and boisterous noise
Spirit so dauntless could not quell ;
Active as they, she guided well,
Check'd and controll'd, yet led the way,
Alike in study and in play.
Chivalric homage soon she won
From those two votaries of fun :
Her wish was held a binding law ;
Shown by a single glance 't would draw

Wild, heedless little Harry back
From folly rash to duty's track,
And strengthen Arthur's sturdier aim
Knowledge to win and future fame.
Each to the other oft confessed
That 'dear Miss Stafford' was the best,
The cleverest, being ever seen,
Fit for an empress or a queen.
Thus pleasantly two years they passed;
Content and useful, Esther cast
Few longing, lingering looks behind,
Nor in the future hoped to find
A deeper joy; her present hours
Fully employ'd her varied powers,
And left her satisfied; but then
Change visited her once again,
This time assuming pleasure's guise,
And sparkling bright before her eyes.
Paterfamilias had to go
To London for a month or so
On business, and resolved to take
With him his family, and make
Business and pleasure once agree,
And view the sights there were to see :
And Esther (who of course went too)
Wild as her pupils almost grew.

Did ever child anticipate
A sight so much as of the great,

Great city?—strange, mysterious theme
For waking thoughts and midnight dream.
Imagination, half in awe,
Its wondrous things attempts to draw
Before the mental eye, but yet
The picture never could complete.
Harry and Arthur never tired
Of its attractions; they admired
In prospect all they were to see
With most enthusiastic glee;
But silence hush'd each youthful voice
When, reaching the metropolis,
Upon it first their vision fell,
While whirling on to their hotel,
And lamps and lighted shops revealed
Much else in mystery conceal'd;
For it was wrapp'd in night's dark shroud.
Esther beheld the living crowd
Rapidly hurrying to and fro,—
A stream that seemed no end to know,
With awe-struck wonder, 'mid a mass
So dense, she thought that she must pass
Unheeded by the Lord of all:
Units must surely be too small
For Him to cherish and protect.
Her doubt His own assurance checked;
Compassionate, the King of kings,
Knowing that human nature clings,

In its dim sight, to unbelief,
For all His little ones' relief,
Told how the very sparrows share
Almighty providence and care.
The sweet remembrance seemed to charm
All Esther's fears to instant calm,
And touch'd her heart's most grateful chords,
While low she spoke the prayerful words—
Words by the world's Redeemer given—
' Our Father ' (our) ' Who art in Heaven.'

Who has not felt that sacred prayer
An overwhelming power to bear,
When uttered 'mid a city's crush ?
Along each clause there seems to rush
A hidden and a deeper thought
Of more significant import.
With reverence may we not compare
Thoughts it suggesteth everywhere
To truth in ordinary type ?
But 'neath the city's light 't is ripe
With fuller meaning ; on the heart
'T is writ in capitals, apart
From earthly rivalries and rights,
Human magnificence and sights
Of kingly splendour far above ;
The praises of the God of love

We offer, in its last grand strains,
Chanted upon the heavenly plains;
For is not such the angels' story,—
' Thine is the kingdom, power, and glory,
For ever and for ever ' ? Then,
Who would not breathe a thrilled ' Amen ' ?

Happy the youthful travellers woke
Next morning, as upon them broke
The glad remembrance where they were,
Giving a most impetuous spur
To toilet operations, while,
Serving their fancies to beguile,
The street cries sounded merrily.
All rules of strict propriety
Their curiosity defied,
And blinds were slightly drawn aside,
Permitting the first daylight peep
At London risen from its sleep.
With earnest haste they soon begun
Their eager pleasure-hunting fun :
Museum, tower, and public mart,
Palace and gardens,—all had part
In their inspection ; but to tell
All that they saw would be to dwell
Upon a theme half tiresome grown,
So wide are London's wonders known.

Suffice it that each rapid day
'Mid strange delights was passed away—
Delights that when recounted o'er
Increased in lustre tenfold more.

Shortly before they left it chanced,
In some excursion, that there glanced
On Esther's face an eye that knew
That face full well ;—its own sweet blue
Deepen'd and brighten'd as across,
To where she stood, sprang Jessie Ross.
Gladly did each the other greet,
Wondering how they chanced to meet ;
But explanations were delayed ;—
Jessie had an appointment made
To meet her brother, and the hour
Was past already ; but before
She left her, it was understood
That the day following Esther should
Spend with her.   Much she seem'd to shun
Giving the promise; but 't was won
From Mrs. Lindsay, who, amused
At seeing Esther so confused,
Fancying she did not like to make
Engagements that might chance to break
Upon arrangements they had made,
Advanced, her modesty to aid,
Frankly insisting she should go,
And hush'd her faintly-spoken ' No. '

Her friend's reluctance Jessie saw,
And, puzzled, from it sought to draw
Conclusions probable, yet wrong :
Had absence she had felt so long
Cool'd Esther's love for friends of youth ?
Or was it nearer to the truth
To guess that her dependence found
Harshness, and that her will was bound
By others' tyranny? And yet
She scarcely thought so when she met
That lady, with her kindly face,
And those bright boys, whose youthful grace
Charm'd her so much ; and so she told
The tale to Donald, to unfold
The mystery. He quickly guessed
The doubt that Esther's mind possessed :
She thought that she should meet him there,
And had not wished it ; so, to spare
Her that annoyance, he would go
On a day's journey, that, although
Important, might have been delayed.
Absent, so long as Esther stayed
Jessie would find her still the same
To her ; he did but merely name
His firm belief that she would find
Esther unchanged in heart or mind ;
That he would have to be away
Most, if not all, the coming day.

Poor simple Jessie never guessed
At hidden motives ; she expressed,
Both then, and on the following morn,
To Esther hopes of his return,
And her vexation he should need
To leave with such immediate speed
That day ; yet, may be, 't was as well,
For each had got so much to tell
The other. Esther's story first
It was agreed should be rehearsed.
Then Jessie told how Donald grew
Noted and rich ; some site to view,
Before he planned, they first had come
To London ; but she longed for home ;
And now not long would be their stay.
Then Esther asked for Cyril Grey,
And who lived at the dear old hall,—
Was it inhabited at all ?
With faltering voice and crimson'd cheek,
Jessie, embarrassed, strove to speak,
Telling her it was empty now.
Of some one, too, she murmur'd low,
Who, renting it, lived there in spring,
And now she thought was purchasing
The whole estate ; again she paused,
While her shy conscious manner caused
Esther some speculative thought,—
Not long, for soon poor Jessie sought

To tell how thereby hung a tale
Of love; but scarce she could prevail
Upon herself the tale to tell—
For she was heroine—but to quell
The quivering at her heart she tried,
With all her might, and then confide
To Esther how Lord Atherton
Came to the hall when first begun
Spring's birds to sing and flowers to bloom,
And from its solitary gloom
Oft to their cottage had repaired,
And walks with her and Donald shared,—
Oftenest with her; what pleasant hours
They spent among their books and flowers.
He was so genial and so kind ;
Well stored, like Donald's, was his mind ;
But he was young, and not so stern,
And it was easier far to learn
From him,—his glad light-hearted way
Made gravest study seem but play.
' T was pleasant very, for she felt
No dread at the deep joy that dwelt,
When he was near, within her heart.
The thought that he must soon depart
Dawned not yet, teaching her to know
She loved him by love's thrilling woe.
She little guessed 't was love, poor child !
That nestled in her heart, and smiled

So brightly, making earth more gay,
Till one sweet afternoon in May
Percy (Lord Atherton) and she
Had wander'd searching merrily
For primroses and violets sweet,
Some miles from home ; her weary feet
Begun to plead at length for rest;
So, turning towards the tinted west,
They sat upon a grassy knoll
Above the lake, and o'er them stole
The calm delicious stillness brings,—
Musings that come on fairy wings
But once or twice ; for bliss so sweet,
Not oft dare mortals hope to greet ;
Joy undefined ; we may not know
What source has made the stream to flow.
But Jessie was to learn the truth,
For as they sat the noble youth,
Fervent, yet shy, commenced to tell
How her sweet presence cast a spell
Of gladness o'er him, erst unknown ;—
An orphan, lonely had he grown
To manhood ; love had cheered him not;
Flatter'd he had been, but his lot
Had been but desolate till now,
When gazing on that candid brow,
And reading in those calm blue eyes—
Whose truthful light knew no disguise—

A sympathy for which he yearned,
Hope for the moment brighter burned
That love would follow; his he gave
Her long before,—to be her slave
And serve her would be dear delight.
But oh ! to be her own loved knight,
To share her smile each precious hour,
And cherish her with all his power—
His honoured wife—she would not say,
Unpityingly and sternly, ' Nay ' ?
What could she say ?—each look and tone
Reveal'd the story of her own
Fond heart, and Jessie realised
How much, how very much, she prized
That deep affection. But anon
·The thought how rank and talent shone
In circles where Lord Percy moved,
Love, hope, and trust alike reproved :
She would disgrace, and vex, and grieve,
And then not long would she receive
Love, that half tempted her to share
A name so noble, and to dare
The world's contempt.   It must not be ;
So, like a child, she guilelessly
Told what she felt, and fear'd, and thought,
And eagerly young Percy sought
To prove her arguments unjust
And groundless.   Would not Jessie trust

His own assurance that there were
In the great world none half so fair,
So charming, noble, and so true
As her sweet self? And, though she knew
Better than trust all he might tell,
Somehow love always will prevail :
Percy won that for which he sighed,
And Jessie was his promised bride.
Donald's consent was soon obtained,—
Glad for his sister ; but it pained
That sister to observe the look
Of weary sadness that he shook
Off when she joined him—all alone,
And desolate, when she was gone.
She grieved for Donald, though he strove
To soothe her by his cheerful love,
And talked of pleasant days in store,
Happier, perchance, than those of yore.

With loving archness Esther heard
Most of the story, nor deferred
Expression of the joy she felt,
Nor of the true warm hopes that dwelt
Within her heart that, as a wife,
Jessie's might be a long glad life.
The marriage day was fixed to be
A few weeks later. Urgently

Jessie besought her friend to come
And spend a while with her at home,
Acting as bridesmaid on the day :
The clergyman was Cyril Grey.
But Jessie pleaded all in vain ;
Esther still urged she must remain
With her young pupils ; none the less
She wished her every happiness ;
Never again she hoped to spend
Such pleasant hours.   Henceforth her friend
Could not be quite so much her own ;
But, to retain when she was gone,
One little golden curl she took,
A theft that Jessie would not brook,
Unless she might herself possess
From Esther's head a light brown tress.

Poor Esther ! As the day wore on
She wished that Donald might return
Before she left ; it might be weak,
But she so longed to hear him speak,
To feel that he forgave the past,
And that in scorn he had not cast
Her wholly from his heart ;—but nay,
Too surely he prolonged his stay.
The carriage came to bear her home,
But he she looked for had not come.
Yes ! But he had, and in the hall
Was waiting there, to hear the fall

Of her light step, and see again
Her who had caused him so much pain.
She met him with a nervous start,
A strange deep yearning at her heart,
And towards him had her hand advanced,
When, thinking of the past, she glanced
Up to his face.   Would he refuse
To take it then ? She could not choose
But see that he looked grey and old,
Indifferent, too, and stern and cold.
Her hand was taken while she looked :
Donald would never have rebuked
Her deeds by rudeness of his own ;
And that short glance to him had shown
That she was pale, subdued, and sad ; —
Her sorrow could not make him glad.
Heavy it weighed upon his heart
As he stood watching her depart,
And every thought of angry scorn
It banished, never to return.

And Esther, she could doubt no more,
If she had had a doubt before,
She loved, and knew it when too late :
Her stubborn pride had seal'd her fate.
Yet through it all she felt a thrill
Of joy, as she remember'd still

That kindlier look and gentle grasp,—
Her hand still seemed to feel its clasp.

Donald and Jessie sat alone,
Talking of what the girls had done
And told each other, when she thought
Of Esther's lock of hair, and brought
It for her brother to admire.
With much of covetous desire,
And loving pride and reverence too,
He drew the little ringlet through
His fingers, thinking whence 'twas shorn,
And who the silken tress had worn.
Jessie looked on with curious eyes,
But great indeed was her surprise
When Donald begged it, with that quick
And high-pitched utterance that would trick
Others to thinking that we mind
Little or nothing, should we find
Refused to us the boon we ask
With such indifference.   Foolish task !
That very light nonchalant air
Often betrays how much we care :
It did to Jessie,—she could trace
Love's autograph on Donald's face ;
And blind and stupid she had been,
She thought, in never having seen
The truth before : she saw it now,
And urged her brother to avow

Her surmise right.   He laid aside
All jesting vain attempts to hide
The struggling passion in his breast;
Slowly and sadly he confessed
Its early growth and changeless strength,
And how he told his love at length.
Of Esther no reproachful word
Or slighting speech his sister heard ;
None, to condemn her, e'er should hear
How he was met with taunt and sneer ;
He merely said his suit was vain,
Not his the power her heart to gain.
Jessie both grieved and wondered too ;
That Esther named him not she knew ;
But, hoping some day she might learn
That Donald's love was worth return,
She gave him half the lock of hair,—
The other half she could not spare.
Contented, he the giver kissed,
And ever after was dismissed
From conversation Esther's name,
Though either heart confessed its claim
To loving memory, and shrined
It in itself with feelings kind ;
But never was allusion made
To what had been that evening said.

The earth its annual circle round
The sun twice more had made, and wound

Some of the threads of mortal life
From out the web; in busy strife
Many were tangled; few were rolled
In smooth straight course and even fold.
Cyril was number'd with the dead—
A crown'd, instead of mitred, head;
Donald was oft obliged to roam
As much in London as at home;
But travel when or where he would,
Finding some means of doing good,
Honour'd for many a noble deed,
Beloved by many a child of need
His hand had help'd, in such a part
Gaining a solace for his heart;
For though the Lord Himself will heal,
And wounded hearts with comfort seal,
Yet, kind and pitiful and just,
Remembering that we are but dust,
He often condescends to bless
By human loves and sympathies.
Jessie, now Lady Atherton,
Thought she quite worldly-wise had grown,
A continental bridal tour
(At court presented, too be sure)
Had made her statelier than before—
Simply in manner, nothing more.
Her childlike heart was still unspoiled,
And still from vanity recoiled.

So peerless was his treasured bride,
We might forgive young Percy's pride.
Esther was sad; the time was come,
She felt, for her to leave the home
Four happy years had rendered dear ;
But duty's path was marked and clear.
She knew 't was time the boys should mix
With other boys, and men should fix
Their studies, subject to the rule
And discipline of public school.
Should she retain her office long,
'T would be to them unjust and wrong ;
So she resigned it—though in dread
Of the dark future o'er her head—
Spite of remonstrance and request,
For she alone believed it best.
The Lindsays, finding it was vain
To urge her stay, much wished to gain
Her some engagement, with as light
And easy duties as they might.
The search required no instant haste,
For Esther longed once more to taste
The breezes by her mountain lake,
And had resolved three months to take
Of quiet holiday ; and then,
Strengthen'd, return to work again.
She meant to lodge (to most unknown)
With her old nurse—a widow lone,

Who from the hall above a mile
Resided now—and there beguile
The pleasant quiet hours away
Of her brief transient holiday.

Adieux were spoken, sad but kind,
And Esther left her friends behind,
Urged ever to regard their home
As hers, and never fail to come
To them when sorrowful or ill,—
There welcome would await her still.
Her letters they agreed to send
To Penrith ; thence a country friend,
Her nurse's son, would bring them on,
For he was often in the town.
He met the stage with his light cart,
And drove her home.   Her weary heart
Beat half with pleasure, half with pain,
As she beheld each sight again
Once so familiar to her eyes,
And saw the whitewashed cottage rise ;
And nurse sat knitting at the door,
Just as she used four years before.
For days a roving life she spent,
And by the lake's still margin went,
Wandering far distant from the cot.
At length she sought a favourite spot,

And sat upon its hilly rise
Till daylight faded from the skies,
And the fair moon shone clear and bright,
And, under cover of the night,
Surveyed her own reflected face
In nature's liquid looking-glass.
Suddenly upon Esther's ear
The sound of oar-strokes drawing near,
Mingled with human voices, fell;
And quickly did her bosom swell,
When 'midst them Donald's voice she heard.
She caught the tone, though not the word—
That rapid eager Scottish tone
Amongst a thousand she had known;
Its rugged sweetness charmed her ear;
No music had been half so dear.
Just then a boat appeared in sight,
And, mid the shadows of the night
She could distinguish figures three,
And almost fear'd that they might see
Her standing there; but it soon passed.
On it one farewell look to cast,
Between the trees she forward bent;
At once the branch on which she leant
Gave way, and, with a startled cry,
She plunged beneath—she thought to die!
It reached the boat, and Donald said
He heard a rustling overhead;

The cry was utter'd in distress,
But whence it came they could not guess.
Wallace was with them in the boat,
So he was quickly ordered out—
Needing no sign, but swimming round
The rock; and Donald, following, found
He held a lady by her dress,
Wrapp'd in complete unconsciousness.
The dog was brave, but growing old,
And scarcely could retain a hold
Of his fair charge, till Donald bore
Her lightly from him to the shore.
Fast onwards to the hall he sped,
Half fearing that the girl was dead,
And vexed to think his house was closed,
Or she might nearer have reposed;
But all the household were away;
His own was just a passing stay,
A week or two, as Jessie's guest;
So faster towards her home he pressed.
Wallace was running by his side,
And whine and caper testified
Some strange emotion that he felt;
But in his master's heart there dwelt
No dim suspicion that his arm
Had rescued from impending harm,
And now encircled, one so dear
As Esther, till, on drawing near

The hall, a light shone on her face,
Revealing to his anxious gaze
The well-known features, pale and still,
So deathlike that he felt a thrill
Of almost terror seize his breast
As close th' unconscious form he pressed.
She had not in the least revived
When Percy and his wife arrived
Up from the boat, amazed to hear
Their guest had proved a friend so dear.
At length she heaved a struggling sigh,
And quick and nervously her eye
Glanced round, as if to question where
She was, and who besides was there.
The glance was followed by a rush
Of recollections, while a blush
With crimson stains suffused her cheek ;
But Jessie would not let her speak,
And lovingly forbade her tell
Even how the accident befel
Till she was rested ; but she knew
'T was easiest then, and so a true
Brief story of the whole she told.
And playfully did Jessie scold
At her desertion of them all ;
But now they held her safe in thrall.
Long her captivity should last
In expiation of the past !

Alarmed at her protracted stay,
Her cottage friends had made their way
Up to the hall, to tell their tale,
And seek for counsel to avail
Them in a search.   They heard, with tears,
Her peril had surpassed their fears.
Jessie protesting that her friend
There her remaining stay must spend,
Listless and faint from weariness
Esther was forced to acquiesce—
More willingly that she perceived
How fully Jessie's plan received
Her husband's sanction : all his face
Was lighted up with kindly grace.
She heard who saved her with a start
Of conscious joy : her foolish heart
Would dwell with pleasure on the thought
That it was Donald; and she sought,
Timidly, as she bade ' Good night,'
To own her grateful thanks aright.
Illness confined her to her room
For many days; though to resume
Her wonted course of life she tried,
Weakness long steadily defied
Her efforts; but she hoped at length
She had regained her former strength,
Bringing from her secluded rest
For social joys a keener zest.

One morning, as she sat alone
With Jessie, somehow talk had grown
More confidential, till it veer'd
Round to a subject each had feared
To touch upon,—the slighted suit
Donald had offered. Esther, mute,
Heard Jessie utter her regret,
And found she knew not all as yet.
Her gentle words pain'd Esther more
Than harsh reproach. A while she bore
It patiently; but illness stole
From her her power of self-control,
And made her suddenly confess,
With much of passionate distress,
Her foolish pride and worthless sneer,
To Jessie's kind forgiving ear.
Her very love she did not hide—
Longer concealment it defied.
She strove less, may be, as she knew
That Jessie's delicate and true
Womanly feeling would compel
Her sacred silence : she would tell
Her confidence to none beside;
But most from Donald would she hide
Its purport; so she frankly told
Her sorrow now, with faults of old.

They knew not in an inner room
Donald sat struggling with the gloom

He felt; and, writing while they spoke,
He heard all; but it strangely woke
No consciousness, until his name
Roused tranquil thoughts to instant flame.
He knew too much to join them then
With easy coolness; but, again,
His room possessed no door but that
Leading to theirs; and so he sat,
Still musing on each tender word
That he so heedlessly had heard,
Almost afraid her love to deem
As other than a blissful dream.

His sister presently was gone;
Esther, he knew, was quite alone.
Should he disclose himself, and ask
Her troth and pardon then, or task
His patience longer, and conceal
Knowledge not meant for him, but seal
His fate by pleading as before?
Loving, she would not, as of yore,
Deny his passionate request.
That course he thought might be the best;
But not for him,—his candid truth
Compell'd confession; so, forsooth,
He went at once and owned the whole,
Vowing that scorn and time had stole

Nought from the fervour of his love,
And urging Esther to remove
The word that severed them so long.
Well did he plead—for hope was strong—
So well that Esther's quivering heart
Yearn'd to consent, till, like a dart,
The past rush'd back upon her view,
And fired her willing pride to sue
For love's subjection, till it gained
Its cause; and as the victor reigned
Within her breast, her words were cold,
From stern compulsion, as she told
Donald that he had heard aright—
She loved, but never would she plight
Her faith while poor, and he contrast
Contemptuous hauteur of the past
With present yielding, and believe
Her love what selfishness might weave—
A worthless fabric. All in vain
Were argument or plea to gain
A different answer;—calm and still,
She conquer'd impulse by her will
(For love with pride had strangely striven),
Though in the strife her heart was riven.
Donald the contest well perceived.
Chafed by her folly, yet he grieved
Sadly, and one last effort made
From her rash purpose to dissuade :—

'Esther, I pray you not to fling
Away our happiness, and bring
A cloud to shade the path of each,
And trouble hearts doubt should not reach,
Merely because when but a child,
By fanciful caprice beguiled,
Scarce old enough to know your heart,
You read its whisp'rings wrong. Apart
From all the past, more justly now,
In pity to us both, allow
My claim for love's dear bond to stand—
Deny me not this priceless hand.'
Reading refusal in her eye,
He did not wait for her reply,—
'I ask it now ; my love would stoop
Even to imploring ; I would droop
All pride myself, and why, oh ! why,
Should yours our happiness defy ?
Esther, again I ask it never—
You will not bid me go for ever ?'
'For ever,' she distinctly spoke,
Though low and hoarse. The words scarce broke
On Donald's ear before he turn'd
And left her, thinking that he spurn'd
A heart so obstinate and proud :
His own with bitterest grief was bow'd.
One step, as if to bid him stay,
Quick Esther moved unseen ; but, nay,—

'T was right, she thought, that he should go;
Wiser it was, and better so,
Though worse than misery to her—
Goading her woe as with a spur.
' For ever' sounded in her ear,
Nought but ' For ever' could she hear,
Till her poor heart could bear no more,
And she sank senseless on the floor.

PART FOURTH.

Youth has few trials more severe,
More harassing, or hard to bear,
Than constant murmurings from the old—
Fretful repinings, that enfold
Each hour of morning, noon, and night,
Weighing on hearts else gay and light.
The quibbling plaint and anxious sigh
Of fretful age would often try
Patience that seldom is bestow'd
On those who in life's rugged road
Have traversed but a few short steps,
Save where some chasten'd spirit reaps,
Even in youth, the holy calm
Of sanctified affliction's balm.
'T is passing strange, we oftenest see
Querulous age where luxury,
And ease, and comfort have been given;
While those who for long years have striven
With hardship, penury, and care,
With self-forgetting cheerful air,
Smile at and share the hopes of youth;
And if forebodings of the truth
Should cross their minds, that thorns may g
And rankle where the roses blow,

Not theirs all present bliss to mar;
Yet none when meeting sorrow are
Readier to lend a helping hand,
Or feel humanity's demand.
Would that such lustre might adorn
Each hoary head by trial worn—
Unfretted though; in perfect love
Resembling spirits crown'd above;
Resting upon the border-land,
Alluring us to that bright strand,
They seek of purity and peace,
Patiently waiting their release;
Fitted themselves, by grace, to dwell
Where everlasting praises swell.

With one far different Esther's lot
Was cast, when hastening from a spot
So fraught with pain as Westmoreland,
And sooner than at first she planned :—
Companion to a stately dame
(Infirm and aged) she became.
'T was all that offer'd, and she seized
It eagerly, though scarcely pleased,
Or by the prospect greatly cheer'd.
Yet worse, far worse, than she had fear'd
She quickly found it; but she bore
With calm indifference all the store

Of railing censure and of sighs,
Scarce heeding them : deep grief defies
The power of little trifling wrongs
And petty stings ; to them belongs
The task of pois'ning happiness :
They pass unfelt by true distress.
Her hopeful heart had lost its spring,
Her joyous fancies taken wing ;
Duty's demands she tried to meet,
Regret and memory to defeat ;
Feeling was lull'd, and sunshine gone ;
And slowly thus the days wore on.

Yet deadlier shadows might surround,
And things be worse, as Esther found
When young Sir Henry Merton came,—
Merton was the old lady's name.
Widow'd, this was her only child ;
But seldom had his presence whiled
Away her solitary hours,
Save when the somewhat dangerous powers
Of creditors, with wrath replete,
Render'd it prudent to retreat
From their displeasure for a while,
And charm the country with his smile.
On such a visit he arrived
Soon after Esther, and deprived

Her of what peace she might have found.
Strife and confusion reigned around
During his tiresome lengthy stay :
Idling he spent each livelong day—
Drinking and swearing at his dogs,
Cursing the dampness of the fogs,
Scolding the servants, with abuse
Loading his mother, who let loose
An angry volley in reply,
With harsh shrill tones and fiendlike eye.
Esther was witness to the whole,
And sometimes scarcely could control
Her deep disgust ; yet greater fear
Oppress'd her when she saw the leer
With which he watched her, or she caught
Looks with coarse admiration fraught.
He strove a friendship to advance
By treating her to jest and glance,
With confidential nods and winks,
From which the heart of woman shrinks
As from a loathsome poison'd air,
That weeds, not fresh sweet flow'rs, should share.

She shunn'd his presence when she might :
It seemed each holy thought to blight ;
Yet perseveringly he talked
On to her still, and often baulked

Her best-laid schemes for solitude.
One day he ventured to intrude
Upon her when, some errand done,
Home from the village she begun
To saunter. Gliding by her side,
Viper-like, much Sir Henry tried,
By complimentary discourse,
His own imagined charms t' endorse,
Though curt the answers and constrain'd
His fashionable lisp obtained.
Esther was not one prone to fear,
But never was Sir Henry near
Than, with an almost nervous dread,
She hastened on with faster tread,
And now had swift her way pursued,
But that it suited not his mood.
Informing her 't was with intent
To meet her there his course was bent,
At once he started to bewail
His lofty station, and to rail
At Providence, or Chance, or Fate ;
Then more succinctly to relate
How love for her such outburst drew—
A love, he vowed, both strong and true,
Strengthen'd by intercourse so sweet ;
And why should pride its course defeat ?
What if his mother's wrath should rise ?—
That he learned long since to despise.

Though old associates, too, might sneer,
His manly courage would not fear.
With much in like heroic strain
He seemed to seek her love to gain ;
While, ere the grand oration closed,
A private marriage he proposed.
Esther was vexed that words too weak
Half her indignant thoughts to speak
Were all that came at her command ;
But even they to fury fann'd
Sir Henry's pompous boastful mind.
Not his the common lot (more kind
Than many think) of being told
His real faults in darkest fold
They were enwrapp'd and hid from view—
At least his own ; but now in true
Clear light before him Esther placed
Meanness and falsehood that disgraced
The name of man.   His rage no bound
Appear'd to know, and soon she found
He might not love, but he could hate ;
And, long or short, no tranquil state
He knew until he trampled low
Those who had dared to aim a blow
At his desires or self-esteem,—
Revenge as certain they might deem.

In Esther's case awhile it stayed—
More to be dreaded since delayed.

On reaching home she soon reveal'd
All to his mother, and appeal'd
To her protection from his rage;
Awaking in that breast of age
Harsh taunting speeches for her son,
And hatred, lasting as his own,
For Esther, though she did not share
The vengeance his wild mind might dare,
If his poor victim he might crush;
Her plan, with yet a heavier rush
Of anger, fretfulness, and spite,
All Esther's harass'd youth to blight.
From it at least one good accrued
(To Esther one of magnitude) —
Sir Henry left his mother's roof,
And held himself a while aloof;
But in a few short months he came
Again its sheltering guard to claim.
This time his plan was all arranged,
And greatly were his habits changed.
His coming marriage he declared,
And gladly all the household shared
His seemingly more gentle mood —
Only to Esther gravely rude,
Watching her with suspicious look,
Whatever course her actions took.
Her desk (now seldom used) he knew—
And that his key unlocked it, too.

And when the others were asleep
To it with stealthiest step he 'd creep,
Jewels and trinkets placing there,
That from his mother's set with care
He took away from time to time.
For charging Esther with the crime
Of theft was what he had devised
As fitting punishment.   Apprised
That one by one her jewels went,
All Lady Merton's thoughts were bent
On finding the offender out;
But, baffled, she could only doubt,
Until she missed a diamond ring,
Costly and rare.   Vowing to bring
The mystery to a sudden close,
She summon'd law to interpose;
And brought its officer to haul
And search at once the goods of all.

Sir Henry ventured to suggest
That probably it might be best
To ascertain who saw it last:
That little clue some light might cast
Upon it; and he deemed 't were well
On that one's property first fell
Investigation. It might chance
Their object greatly to advance.

To all 't was known that Esther's eye
Had been the last the ring to spy,
When bringing Lady Merton down
A brooch she wanted : it was gone
When next the casket was surveyed
By Antoinette, the lady's maid.
Esther was conscious of the slight
Sir Henry's words convey'd ; and might
Her innocence be fully proved,
And that strange stigma be removed,
Resolved a more congenial home
To seek, though far she had to roam.
All she possess'd was ransack'd o'er,
Except her desk.   Sir Henry wore
A haggard, nervous, pallid look,
His hand, too, somewhat slightly shook,
When, having placed it in their view,
Towards it he fresh attention drew.
But—little guessing that his hand
Had touched, and oft his eye had scanned,
Each content, that a sacred thing
She held—quick Esther made a spring
Forward, with the impulsive plea,
' Oh ! not my desk !' in time to see
The missing jewels all disclosed.
Those who unshaken trust reposed
In her till then now stood aloof,
Stagger'd by such convincing proof.

Swift 'cross her mind there flash'd the thought
By whom the treachery was wrought;
Calm and collected, she perceived
The well-laid plot; nor more deceived
Was Lady Merton. Well she knew
Her son would ruthlessly pursue
A triumph that she strove to aid,—
Of his detection most afraid.
That night within the county gaol
Esther was lodged; of no avail
Was it that she disclaim'd the deed:
The facts were thought too strong to need
More confirmation; so she pent
Her heart's deep anguish up, and bent
Prostrate to let them work their will,
Cold as a statue and as still.

The story soon appeared in print:
Thus it was Donald gained a hint
Of the affair; his trustful mind
No doubt of Esther's truth enshrin'd.
Puzzled and grieved he was indeed,
But of her suffering and her need
He only thought;—his was the right
To soothe and cheer her; and ere night
Set in, his journey was begun—
Trusting that Esther would not shun

His sympathy in her distress,
His aid in seeking some redress.

Thick fell the large white flakes of snow,
And winds were moaning out their woe,
As, on a dark December morn,
Deserted, hopeless, and forlorn,
Esther sat crouching in her cell,
Crush'd 'neath the blow that on her fell
So suddenly ; her heart felt cold,
As prison'd in an icebound hold,
And hope and joy and grief had fled,—
Pride and resentment too were dead.
Her thoughts were free to range the past,
But fetter'd if a glance they cast
On present or on future things—
Like to a harp whose broken strings
Only admit a trifling part
Of its wild whisp'rings to the heart.
No feeling seem'd her soul to thrill,
Except it might be terror's chill,
As footsteps sounded 'long the floor,
And the key turn'd within the door ;
And no emotion or surprise
Appear'd by outward sign to rise
When Donald entered there alone.
Rigid and motionless as stone,

She watched him with a steady gaze
Advance, and suffered him to raise
Her up and kiss her pale worn cheek ;
But neither had the power to speak.
He drew her head on to his breast,
And long 't was silently caressed ;
While Esther, clinging to his arm,
As if there only safe from harm,
Had locked the floodgates of her grief—
Words would not come to give relief.
Thus nearly half an hour had passed,
Gliding too surely and too fast,
When towards them heavy footsteps sped ;
And in an agony of dread
She lifted up her shackled wrist,
Their separation to resist.
' Donald, don't leave me, do not go ! '
She pleaded heedless of the woe
That echoed in her bitter cry ;
If left, she felt it was to die.
Donald had been to offer bail
Before he visited the gaol :
His own and Percy's name obtained
Acceptance of it,—so he gain'd
Freedom for Esther till the time
Fixed for the trial of the crime.
He knew not now how much to tell,
If but that she must leave, as well,

Unquestioning she would receive
What he should say, and might believe
That truth had won the victory,
And hope that she was wholly free.
Details he feared might give her pain,—
And that his tenderness was fain
To spare her wounded breaking heart;
So he strove gently to impart
The real truth, and yet suppress
Terms that might waken her distress.
Well Esther understood the whole:
Feeling was roused, and teardrops stole
Fast from her eyes, while burning came
To her fair cheek the blush of shame.
Confinement in that hideous place,
The degradation and disgrace,
She knew but scarce had felt before;
The scene now all its horrors wore
Before a gaze intensified;
And, almost wishing she had died,
Her face 'gainst Donald's arm she hid,
Till fainting from its clasp she slid.
The pang that forces human grief
To words or tears oft brings relief;
And Esther felt, when she revived,
Her sorrow's outburst had deprived
That sorrow of its keenest hold.
Her face seem'd more of mortal mould,

And less like rigid sculptured stone,
While somewhat lighter, too, had grown
The heavy weight upon her heart,
That might not all at once depart.

Confiding all to Donald's care,
She drove,—but never asking where—
With him, miles distant from the gaol,
By far too stricken and too frail
To plan her course or make request
What Donald will'd would be the best.
Supposing Jessie's home to be
Their destination, silently
And long she ponder'd should she find
Her still the same, or might her mind
Be warp'd by doubt: she could not say.
But when her grief the heaviest lay
Full faith in Donald's trust she felt;
Within her heart had constant dwelt
The sweet assurance he would ne'er
Leave her alone deserted there;
Proofs might be many and be strong,
He'd hold her guiltless of the wrong
Of Jessie she was not so sure ;
She felt she never could endure
From her a doubting glance to meet ;
But scarcely was the thought complete,

Ere all its bitterness and fear
Were whispered into Donald's ear,
And, all unasked, she tried to tell
How every circumstance befel.
To him this once she would declare
Her innocence of any share
In the strange theft of which he knew,
Though tears of shame the effort drew.
Donald was glad at length to gain
Her confidence; to her, 'twas plain,
Without that aid his faith stood fast,
Firm and enduring to the last.
Again the sound of Jessie's name
From Esther questioningly came,
And with a strange surprise she heard
Her friend had never learned a word
Of the event: Lord Atherton
And she to Italy were gone
Ere it occurred.   With puzzled air,
Esther next asked of Donald where
He meant to take her ?—she had thought
The hall had been the home they sought.
With tenderness, resolved and grave,
Donald his answer calmly gave,—
Home to the cottage !   Hastily
Unfolding them, he let her see
A marriage licence and a ring ;
Less than an hour, he said, would bring

Them to a village, where he stayed
In going, and arrangements made
From their home-course an hour to spare,
And take the marriage vows while there
That morning.   Well did he maintain
An air of confidence, to gain
His end, and yet 't was little felt.
Meanwhile in Esther's bosom dwelt
Conflicting thoughts she scarce could guide
Or regulate, though much she tried.
Sorrow had taught humility,
And love was echoing Donald's plea;
She seemed to rest upon his strength,
And yearn'd to have a right at length
His counsel and his aid to claim;
While separation's very name
Tortured her heart.   Yet could she bear
His name in her disgrace to wear?
Her pride before had done him wrong,
That to repair she had not long,
For life she felt was ebbing fast;
'T were sweet to spend it to the last
With Donald, and she judged him well
In guessing how his heart would swell
With rapture, and would sternly fling
Aside the world's disdain and bring
Solace to hers;—that time would be
His one most cherished memory.

When she was gone it might impart
Some comfort to his suffering heart.
So with his wishes she complied,—
Wishes so oft before denied.
Hiding forebodings in her breast,
She every other thought confessed,
And sought forgiveness of the pride
So long permitted to divide
Hearts closely knit in bonds of love.
Sadly she mused, as Donald strove
(Hope shining brightly from his eyes
At all they were to realise)
To picture years of happiness;
Her heart ached with the consciousness
That near and heavy was the blow
Visions so fair were doomed to know.

Ere long the village church they gained.
Within a peaceful stillness reigned.
No agitation marked the look
Or tone of either as they took
Those holy vows; but calm they knelt
Before the altar, while there dwelt
In both a precious trusting faith—
Dearer than life, more strong than death.
The rite was ended: Donald raised
His wife up lovingly, and gazed

Upon her face.   To him it seem'd
The glance of tenderness that gleam'd
From her clear eyes so pure and fair
Was such as angels' looks might wear.
But let us veil an hour replete
With sacred confidence, and greet
The trav'llers as their home they neared
By night;—a myriad stars appear'd,
Shining above the mountain ridge,
While in a boat from Pooley Bridge
Quickly along the lake they rowed.
'T was Christmas Eve, and feeling glow'd
Grateful and strong as Esther thought
Of Bethlehem and the love that brought
Christ to redeem a sinful race
Of ruined men : what wondrous grace
Were in His life and death combined !
Then faith glanced forward, till her mind
Rested upon the peace, the love,
The bliss awaiting her above—
Bliss Donald very soon would share.
That thought made all the rest more fair;
And closer to his side she drew,
As earthward then a glance she threw,
And thoughts of death and parting came,
To wake a sigh that few could blame.
Lights from the cottage now were shown,
The waters, too, had shallower grown,

And almost in a moment more
She stood with Donald on the shore,
In childhood trodden and beloved.
Why had her footsteps ever roved?
They never more should wand'ring roam
From this her own and Donald's home.
Nursing, and tenderness, and skill
Were given her there, but prosper'd ill:
Weaker, more shadowy, day by day
She seemed to grow, and anguish lay,
Fighting with hope, in Donald's heart;
If aught could bid the stain depart
That rested upon deeds so pure
As hers, he thought 't would work a cure
The most effectual, so he drew
Forth all his energy and threw
It to the work.   Alas! in vain,—
The charge seem'd only strength to gain.
The Lindsays spurn'd it, and their aid
Was given to Donald; but, afraid
Of agitating Esther more,
The aspect that the matter wore
Was hidden from her; till one day,
As she was sitting near the bay
Talking with Donald, news was brought,
Officially, of strange import:—
Sir Henry Merton had been slain
In duelling; while he had lain,

In terror at the point of death,
He pleaded with his gasping breath
To see a magistrate.   They brought
One to his presence, and he sought
Distinctly to relate the wrong
Esther had suffered from so long.
His scheme of vengeance and his deed
Of crime confess'd entirely freed
Her from suspicion ; but too late,—
Sorrow and shame had seal'd her fate.
The eyes were tearful that she raised
To Donald's ; he had fondly gazed,
Trusting to see the healthful spring
Of life, that hope revived should bring ;
But in those clear sweet eyes he read
The withering, blighting truth instead—
That waning was her mortal life,
Fast, very fast.   His gentle wife
Knew what it was that he perceived,
And for his agony she grieved.
Each knew the other's thought as well
As if expressed in words it fell
Upon the ear ; but neither spoke,
Save when from Esther quivering broke
Some word of soothing tenderness,
Answer'd by fond, but mute, caress.

Donald possessed a power of will
Not often found, and stronger still

Was love for Esther ; so he vowed
He would not let his misery cloud
Her parting life ;—love, only love,
Then should it be her lot to prove
He vowed, and well he kept it long,
Striving ' to suffer and be strong.'
But once the tempest in his soul
Burst forth, in spite of all control,—
A hurricane of passion's tide.
The anguish, for so long denied
A voice, now bitter accents wrung ;
And to his lips despairing sprung
Words filling Esther with dismay,—
To comfort him, what could she say ?
She thought that what had brought relief
To her might soothe her husband's grief,
And help him to endure the stroke ;
So grave and quietly she spoke :—

' When first I knew that I must die,
    Donald, my heart was wrung
With dread and darksome agony,
    And fast to life I clung ;
Till one day, as I sorrowed thus,
    Distinct I seemed to hear
The Saviour's kind upbraiding voice,
    Speaking in accents clear :—

' " Esther, you were not used to spurn
    The messages I sent,
Or from My loving gifts to turn,
    Or blessings that I lent ;
But now I send My messenger,
    To bring you safely home,
You will not listen to the voice,
    But, lingering, wish to roam !"

' I pleaded earth was beautiful,
    I could not quit my hold,
And death seem'd very terrible—
    I fear'd its icy cold.
Why had we sunshine, flowers, and spring,
    To twine around the heart,
Making it tighter earthward cling ?—
    We had so soon to part.

' He said, " Yes, earth is beautiful ;
    My hand its surface bless'd
With joys you fain would stay to cull ;
    But heavenly joys are best.
To those who all their sacred bliss
    Are privileged to find
Remembrance of the former things
    Shall never come to mind.

· " The flowers of that eternal spring
　　　Under no curse are laid ;
Earth's, while they seem so flourishing,
　　　Are almost seen to fade.
Here sunshine, even when 't is seen,
　　　Is but a passing light ;
Heaven's is a clear enduring beam.—
　　　There naught is known of night."

' I listened, and my weary heart
　　　Almost inclined to go,
For well I knew that trouble oft
　　　Was felt by those below.
But, then, life's dearest, strongest claim
　　　Came rushing on my heart ;
And, as I breathed my husband's name,
　　　I prayed we might not part.

' But oh ! the sight of Jesu's love,
　　　That then to me was given—
Surpassing, dearest, even yours—
　　　It made me long for Heaven.
And yet, and yet—may God forgive !—
　　　But, Donald, even then
Shadows seemed resting on its joys
　　　Till we should meet again.

'Compassionate the Saviour spoke,
  And bade me not to grieve,
For He would guard and bless the one
  That I so fear'd to leave—
Leading us both by paths unknown,
  If thorny, yet to meet
In happiness before His throne,
  And worship at His feet.

'Life, death, and thee I now can trust
  Entirely to Him,
So kind, so merciful, and just—
  So gracious to redeem.
And Donald, dear one, tell me that
  You would not have me stay ;
Jesus will heal your wounded heart
  When I have passed away.'—
But, 'May He help me to submit !'
  Was all that heart could say.

The day was breaking one sweet morn
In spring, and breezes light were borne,
A widely-opened casement through,
Into a room, where Esther drew
Faintly and slow her failing breath.
No need to ask if that were death !

It was her birthday—twenty-three
Were all that she had lived to see.
This was the last; its sunshine bore
Thoughts back to one seven years before,
When gay they went to Aira Force ;—
It still roll'd on with accents hoarse,
But Esther's course was almost run,
Less sparkling than when first begun ;
But such the clear pure calm displayed,
It seemed far loveliest in the shade.
The watchers spoke not,—all was hush'd
In silence, but there often rush'd
'Cross Esther's watchful dying gaze
A look of love she sought to raise
To Donald, and his hand was fast
Clasp'd by her own till life was past.
So still, so peacefully, it fled,
They scarcely knew that she was dead.

Alone beside her Donald knelt,
Heedless to hide the grief he felt ;
It could not hurt her; but it seem'd
As if the perfect peace that beam'd
Even in death from that fair face
Forbade his woe ;—he could but trace
Her upward flight; now she was bless'd
Unutterably, and at rest.

Sunbeams that pierced that darken'd room
He did not feel to mock his gloom :
They seemed to typify the light
Then bursting upon Esther's sight.
Not his the wish to bring her back ;
But often as the lone dark track,
Spread out before him, met his view,
In prayer and faith he sorrowing drew
Close to the tender loving Arm
That sheltered her so safe from harm.
Even as they laid her 'neath the sod,
Heart-broke, he tried to kiss the rod.

Distant he wandered from the spot,
And both had been long time forgot ;
For nearly fifty years had flown :
Old men were dead, and boys were grown
To grandsires, when a stranger came
(An aged man of unknown name)
To the old cot ; his step was slow,
Infirm, and feeble ; white as snow
His locks of hair ; but travel's dye
Had stained his cheek ; his full dark eye
Shone with the lustre of his youth,
And told of nobleness and truth.
The children watch'd him day by day
Visit the place where Esther lay ;

But intercourse with none he sought,
Save when some kindly deed he wrought.
He linger'd kneeling there so still
One day that, fancying he was ill,
Shily the little ones drew near ;
But with a strange alarm and fear
Back to their homes they swiftly fled,
To tell them there that he was dead!
It was too true ; but none could tell
His name, or where his friends might dwell ;
So the old clergyman was brought,
And his decisive counsel sought.
He had succeeded Cyril Grey,
And glancing on the form that lay
Before him, wrapt in Death's embrace,
Instantly knew the speaking face
Of Donald Ross.   The weary strife
And sorrow of his lonely life
Were over—and in Esther's grave
The wished-for resting-place they gave.
There a small tombstone used to rise,
Sometimes attracting strangers' eyes:
But mosses now and lichens hide
Its record that they lived and died.

THE END.